Emily Upham's
REVENGE

A Massachusetts Adventure by
AVI

ILLUSTRATED BY PAUL O. ZELINSKY

Morrow Junior Books

New York

J

≈ *For Emily* ≈

10 9 8 7 6 5 4 3 2 1

The poem "Don't Tell a Lie" is from a popular book of poetry
of the period, *Mrs. E. P. Miller's Mother Truth's Melodies:
Common Sense for Children*

Library of Congress Cataloging-in-Publication Data
Avi, 1937-
Emily Upham's revenge, or, How Deadwood Dick saved the banker's
niece: a Massachusetts adventure / by Avi; pictures
by Paul O. Zelinsky
p.   cm.
Summary: During the summer of 1875, a seven-year-old girl is sent
to live with her wealthy uncle in Massachusetts and becomes involved
in a very suspicious bank robbery.
ISBN 0-688-11898-4
[1. Robbers and outlaws — Fiction. 2. Massachusetts — Fiction.]
I. Zelinsky, Paul O., ill.   II. Title.   III. Title: Emily Upham's
Revenge.   IV. Title: How Deadwood Dick saved the banker's niece.
[PZ7.A 953Em   1992b]
[Fic] — dc20   92-390
CIP
AC

Contents

1 · ESCAPE!   1

2 · DEADWOOD DICK TO THE RESCUE!   21

3 · THE BODY ON THE RAILS!   45

4 · MYSTERIOUS STRANGER!   64

5 · DISCOVERY   71

6 · GREAT BANK ROBBERY   84

7 · IN PURSUIT!   101

8 · TRAPPED!   116

9 · BY DARK OF NIGHT!   139

10 · EMILY UPHAM'S REVENGE!   157

Note

Emily Upham believes that none of the following would have happened if her father had not said *that* word.

ESCAPE!

In the summer of 1875 Emily Upham's father was in a fair way to being ruined. Desperately in need of money for his business, he said that if it came to it, he would even steal. His wife begged him not to speak so wildly, especially in front of his daughter, Emily, who was only seven.

"It is not dignified for a gentleman to say such things," said Emily's mother.

It was then that Emily heard *that* word.

"It's money I need and money I'm going to get," her father shouted. "Dignity be *damned!*"

Emily was horrified. Trembling, she fled to

her room and flung herself upon her knees. There she prayed very hard to God that He would not punish her father for saying such an awful word.

Alas, the very next morning her father had gone, leaving only a note. It read: *When I get money I'll come back.*

That afternoon, Emily's mother became ill. The doctor said it was nerves, that she needed rest, that she must try to get out of the city. Immediately, Emily's mother wrote to Emily's uncle.

This uncle was George P. Upham, brother of Emily's father. But since the brothers did not like one another, Emily had never seen him, not even once. A banker, Uncle Upham lived in North Brookfield, a small town in central Massachusetts.

Three days after Emily's mother sent *her* letter, Uncle Upham answered with *his* letter. It read: *If my brother has gone to the devil, then both you and his daughter had best join him.*

Emily's mother cried that she would never be a poor relation and beg for charity. "It does not matter what happens to me," she said through her tears, "but the Uphams *must* take care of Emily!" If necessary, she proclaimed, Emily would go to her uncle—alone.

After that, things happened very quickly.

On Monday Emily's mother wrote back to Uncle Upham, informing him that Emily *would* arrive at North Brookfield on Friday afternoon, no later.

On Tuesday she ordered the Boston house closed up.

On Wednesday she fired all servants save Polly.

On Thursday she spent the entire day crying.

Nevertheless, on Friday morning Emily's mother shut the door of the Boston house and gave Polly just enough money with which to purchase a ticket to North Brookfield.

"Emily," said her mother, "do not speak to strangers. But, if you must do so, remember that you are a lady. Try not to get excited, Emily. Excitement is not good for little girls. But, if you do become excited, close your eyes and count to fifteen. It always helps."

Then, fondly kissing her daughter on both cheeks, Emily's mother went off to her own sister's country house. Polly took Emily to the train station and bought her the necessary ticket. After this, Emily, along with her trunk, her traveling bag, and her parasol, was placed on the train.

As they were waiting for the train to depart, Polly became more and more worried about her young charge.

"Miss Emily," she finally said, "don't you think you had better come stop with me? Sure, it doesn't seem right to send you off alone this way. I'm mortally certain it's a wild place you're going to, with strange people and stranger animals roaming about."

Emily was shocked. "Polly, do you mean that I would go to *your* house?" she asked.

This made Polly look at Emily in a way that she had never looked at her before, though she had taken care of the girl day and night for all of Emily's seven years. It was a look that almost made Emily sorry she had said anything.

"And is my house not good enough for you, Miss Emily?" asked Polly.

Emily began to find it hard to breathe. "My mama," she managed to speak, "said I was to go on the train. My uncle, who is George P. Upham,

"I'm mortally certain it's a wild place you're going to ..."

banker at North Brookfield, will be waiting for me."

"So your mother did say," said Polly as the train blared its final warning whistle. "And may the Lord bless your voyage." Turning quickly, Polly left the car.

Moments later, the train carrying Emily Upham moved out of Boston station on its way to North Brookfield.

In North Brookfield, Seth Marple sat upon the steps of his home reading a crumpled, yellow-backed dime novel titled *Deadwood Dick as a Boy, or, Why Wild Ned Harris, The New England Farm Boy, Became the Western Prince of the Road.*

Just as Seth was finding out how Deadwood, his favorite hero, was managing to rescue a runaway Italian princess from a band of Mohawk Indians, the Reverend Abraham Farnlee's wagon, mule in harness, came down the road.

Preacher Farnlee was not a problem. But with him were Mr. Marryat, Sheriff Bliss, *and* Mr. George P. Upham. When Seth saw that, he dropped his book and fled into the house.

Inside the small wooden building Seth's mother was kneading bread, but Seth dared not stop to talk. Even as a knock came upon the door he dove into the back closet, pulled the door shut, and latched it from the inside.

"Mrs. Marple," asked the preacher, "is your son to home?"

The Reverend Abraham Farnlee was no stranger to the Marple house. Ever since Seth's father died three years before, the preacher often came to see Mrs. Marple, who was considered winsome and worthy by those who made such judgments. Usually the preacher talked about Christian missionary work in the South Seas. He also tried to be nice to Seth, providing him with Sunday school tracts such as *Improving Stories for the Young*. Seth paid him and the tracts little mind.

Mrs. Marple, looking at the four men who stood in her doorway, hastily wiped the flour from her hands. "He's in the closet, Mr. Farnlee," she replied in an alarmed whisper.

"Please forgive me," said the preacher politely. Walking across the room, he tried to open the closet, only to find it latched shut.

Seth, who had a very good idea of what was coming, set to work at the back of the closet, pulling at the wall boards in the hope of making an escape.

"Seth!" cried Mr. Farnlee, addressing the door, "you are in grave trouble, the kind of trouble I would not put upon a South Seas heathen."

Seth, knowing that the preacher saved his worst for South Seas heathens, applied extra strength and pulled the first board loose.

"We must discuss a certain matter, Seth," Mr. Farnlee continued to speak to the door. "A little politeness and respect would be wise. Think of your poor mother."

Seth started on a second board.

"Is there any way out of the closet?" demanded Mr. Upham.

George P. Upham, North Brookfield's banker and the richest man around, was more feared than loved. Everybody owed him money, a fact that allowed him to act as if he owned the town. Everywhere he went he carried a big black box with a lock attached to it. In the box he kept his accounts. Whenever he met someone who owed him money, which was often, he took out his key, opened the box, and told that person exactly what was owed.

"It is just a closet, Mr. Upham," said Mrs. Marple.

"Seth Marple!" shouted the banker. "You may stay there if you like; we intend to do right by the citizens of North Brookfield!" And turning to the man next to him, he said, "Mr. Marryat, speak your piece!"

"This past week," promptly began Mr. Marryat, the local postmaster, "I was tending to necessary chores, so I could not rightly deliver the mail myself. I hired that boy in there, Seth Marple, to deliver it. It was charity," he added, with a nod toward the preacher.

"Was not!" shouted Seth from inside the closet. He had gotten the second board loose. "Ten cents for fifteen hours' work ain't charity. It's thieving!"

"But after a few days," the postmaster went on with his story, paying the boy as little attention as he did salary, "people started complaining about not getting any mail. 'The boy was supposed to deliver,' says I. 'Never came,' says they.

Then Mr. Upham himself came to complain."

"I haven't received a single letter this past week," acknowledged the banker. "And I have important business to conduct," he added, thumping his black accounts box.

"Well," continued the postmaster, "*that* was serious. I asked the boy about it. 'Don't know anything,' says he. 'You're sure?' says I. 'Not a bit,' says he. 'Stealing the mail of the United States of America is a heinous crime,' says I. 'Ten cents is worse,' says he. So I set Sheriff Bliss here to spy out the boy. What say you, Mr. Bliss?"

"When Mr. Marryat told me his suspicions," confessed Mr. Bliss, North Brookfield's sheriff, "I hoped for the best. I always do. All the same, madam, Mr. Upham, gentlemen, I followed the boy the next morning. He had a packet of letters in his hand. Well, madam, Mr. Upham, gentlemen, he took them out along the creek—past the mill, you see—folded them up into boats, and set them a-sailing. Every one of the letters sank. The truth, plain and simple, madam, Mr. Upham, gentlemen, is that Seth Marple sank the U.S. mail."

Mrs. Marple sighed.

Seth got the third board loose.

"Are you aware," bellowed Mr. Upham, thumping his black box, "that I have been cut off from all communication with the outside world this past week?"

"Weren't fair wages," Seth cried out, edging the third board out and grabbing hold of a fourth.

"Hold your tongue," the banker roared.

"Think of the hereafter, Seth," pleaded Mr. Farnlee.

"I'm working on it now," Seth answered, as the fourth board came out.

"Seth Marple," cried the Reverend Mr. Farnlee to the door, "it pains me to say this before your devoted mother, but you have been a problem to the good people of North Brookfield. This is not the first time we have had to call. Destroying the mail is a dreadful act. It is in our power to send you to the workhouse, though I assure you, that is no wish of mine. What have you to say for yourself?"

Seth had his feet through the hole. "It's all Mr. Upham's fault and no more!" he yelled.

Seth's remark caused the banker to lose his

temper. "Send him to the workhouse! That'll teach him. That's the decision of *this* committee!"

"Think about your dear mother," cried Mr. Farnlee.

"Come out, Seth." Mrs. Marple's voice joined the others. "You must listen to these men."

"Come out, boy," screamed the banker, "or I'll skin you alive!" So saying, Mr. Upham put his account box on the floor, placed his hands on the closet door, set himself, and pulled. It made an awful rip.

The door now stood open. Four men peered into the closet, but they saw nothing except a hole in the back wall. Seth Marple was running split-lickety down the road.

Emily Upham remained in her seat; in fact, she had hardly moved at all during the six hours she had traveled. Still wearing her white gloves, she kept her eyes focused directly to the front. She had placed her traveling bag on one side, her parasol on the other. She had answered questions with no more than a "Yes" or a "No" the entire way.

The locomotive whistle blew long and low, long and low, then let out a short shriek.

The conductor hurried down the aisle. "If you're certain, miss, that North Brookfield is your stop, this be it."

Emily did not even look at him. She was upset that her white pinafore had become smudged with traveling soot. And in her reflection in the window, at which from time to time she stole glances, she could see that her hair, which Polly had brushed to a brilliant shine, was not as it should be. Worse than that, her high collar, long sleeves, and button shoes all conspired to make her both hot and uncomfortable.

"Is someone meeting you?" the conductor asked.

"Yes," Emily whispered, wishing he would not speak so loudly.

The train whistle blew a fourth time, announcing that they were getting even closer. Emily's heart began to beat faster.

"North Brookfield! North Brookfield!" roared the conductor, passing down the aisle.

Hissing and puffing steam and smoke at every hole, the locomotive slowed even more.

Emily closed her eyes, counted to fifteen, then rose. The brakes squealed, bringing the train to a stop. Her bag in one hand, her parasol in the other, Emily made her way cautiously down the aisle.

The conductor threw down the metal steps of the loading platform with a crash. Then he jumped to the ground, turned, and offered Emily his hand. Refusing it, Emily took one step at a time until she stood on North Brookfield's station.

It was not much of a station. The tracks ran through a gully; on either side of it the ground, covered with bushes and trees, rose up sharply. The dirt road that came down to the station ran along the tracks, passed the station house, then stopped, as if to suggest that having done its duty by coming so far, it would not go an inch farther.

The station house was a three-sided wooden hut with a dirty bench along its back wall. Upon its side hung a sign:

NORTH BROOKFIELD

Emily was the only passenger to get off the train. Worse, nobody was there to meet her.

The conductor read her thoughts. "This *is*

your stop, miss," he told her. "Just as your ticket said. North Brookfield, sure enough."

Down the line, her trunk was hoisted out and set upon the road.

"You sure someone's going to meet you?" the conductor asked in friendly fashion.

"My uncle," Emily replied softly, "is George P. Upham, Banker."

The conductor touched his hat in salute. "Good enough, miss. Just wanted to be sure." So saying, he waved his arm at the engineer, who was peering at him from the locomotive cab. " 'Board!" shouted the conductor.

A black puff of smoke shot out of the engine's stack. The locomotive chuffed once, then twice. Cars creaked. Couplings banged. The whole train began to move down the line. The noise was deafening.

"Good luck to you and your banker uncle!" cried the conductor as he swung onto the train.

Emily remained looking after the train until she could see it no longer. For a second she thought she heard the sound of a wagon behind her, but when she looked around, she saw she was mistaken.

She turned in the direction of the departed train. Even the smoke was gone. She looked back toward Boston. Empty also. She looked across the tracks. Bushes and trees, much the same as on her side, met her eyes.

Emily stood for as long as possible, but not even the parasol over her head could keep the heat away. Though it made her feel ill to do so, she went into the wooden hut and sat down.

Putting her traveling bag on one side of her feet, her parasol on the other, she folded her white gloved hands neatly in her lap. There was nothing to do but wait—and attempt to keep from crying.

Seth Marple loped along the dirt road in his bare feet at a steady pace, cursing Mr. Upham. As far as he was concerned, the other men did not really matter. Only after the banker had complained did the others join in.

Seth knew where he was going. He had built a hideout in a place in the woods where hardly anyone ever went. He used it whenever he needed to get away, which was often enough. No one knew about it, not even his mother. It was just down the road over which he was running, just a cut over an unused field and a turn by a broken tree. What he would do when he reached it, he hadn't decided. Except for one thing: he had to stay out of North Brookfield for a time.

A sudden clatter made him look back. The preacher's wagon was fast approaching. On the box was Mr. Upham, cracking the whip over the mule as if he were chasing the Devil himself. Next to him, holding tightly to the seat, was Mr. Farnlee.

"Stop!" cried the banker. "By order of the law, I command you to stop!"

Seth needed but one look. Off he flew, running as fast as he could, knowing he could no longer get to his hideout. They would follow him there for certain.

As he ran he heard the long, low whistle of the four o'clock Boston–Albany train passing through. It hardly ever stopped in North Brookfield.

Then he heard a short, shrieking whistle. The train *was* going to stop. Someone was getting on or getting off.

In the instant Seth heard the stop whistle he

made his decision: as the train paused, he would get on it. He would be halfway to Albany before banker Upham could begin to look for him.

Ahead of Seth were the side road that dropped down into the gully and the tracks where the station hut had been built. And from the sounds of the train, his timing was right. He could catch the cars just as they began to pull out. Seth looked back over his shoulder one final time.

The banker was pumping the whip. The wagon was gaining. The preacher was calling out, "Seth, for your mother's sake, stop!"

Seth did nothing of the kind. Spinning down the side road, he shot into the gully. His foot snagged a rock and down he went into a three-somersault dive. Picking himself up, he pressed on.

The train was about to leave. It had sounded its departing whistle.

Seth skidded down to the tracks so fast that he could hardly breathe. But he had missed the train; it was moving out. Worse luck, as he hit the bottom of the gully he saw someone, back toward him, standing by the tracks.

Seth didn't break stride. He dove into the

bushes, then raced back up the gully and through the bushes toward the road. Reaching the top, he jammed to a stop.

"The fool's caught the train!" It was the booming voice of banker Upham.

Seth stood still.

"Then there's no use going after him," suggested the preacher with relief. "He'll be gone by now."

"Good riddance is what I say," cried the banker. "We're better off without him. Now, Mr. Farnlee, I know you've got your heart set on that Marple widow, so you're better off without the boy too. Mind, if he shows up again, I won't stand for any nonsense. Come on, I need a drink."

Seth watched the banker turn the wagon around and head back toward town. When he was certain that the two men had gone, he slid down the gully.

2

DEADWOOD DICK
TO THE RESCUE!

Seth lay unmoving at the bottom of the gully. His head was pounding, and it hurt just to draw air. But Seth, feeling safer with every passing moment, allowed himself time.

"Won't ever come back," he said to himself. "I'll become rich and buy 'em out. Be an outlaw out West. Be Deadwood Dick. Get killed and make 'em sorry." He listed a long string of particulars, all of which amounted to the notion that he would do *something*.

As he lay there he remembered that he had seen someone standing by the tracks. It had to be the person for whom the train had stopped. And it was reasonable to suppose that if someone got off the train, someone else was going to come and fetch them.

Rolling over onto his stomach, Seth snaked up to the edge of the bushes and looked. Not a soul was there; all he saw was a large trunk. Seth studied it. It was quite the biggest trunk he had ever seen, big enough so that he could have fitted inside it. But nobody was with the trunk at all. The person, he decided, must be sitting in the station shack.

Seth tried to recollect if he had heard talk about someone coming to town. North Brookfield was such a small place that there would have been gossip if anyone was expected. But he could not recall anything. He wondered who had arrived.

Hunched up bullfrog fashion, Seth counted to three, then shot out across the tracks and leaped head first into the bushes on the other side. He moved up along the tracks, always keeping behind bushes for safety's sake. Only when he had gone far enough to have a clear view of the hut did he pull away the branches and take a look inside.

It was a girl.

The girl was dressed all in white; she even wore white button shoes. She had long glossy black hair and the palest face he had ever seen. But the greatest puzzle was that she didn't move. Seth wasn't even certain if she was alive until he saw a big tear roll down her cheek.

Seth sat back on his heels.

Emily felt as though she had been waiting for hours. Once or twice she thought she heard someone, but nobody came. Where, she kept asking herself, was Uncle Upham? She almost wished that she *had* gone to Polly's house.

What she hoped most was that another train would come along. If a conductor saw her, a young lady in distress, he would take her back to Boston and return her to her mama. But nothing came of her wishes.

In the midst of her wishing, hoping, and praying, she spied something moving in the bushes directly opposite to where she was sitting. It was only a little movement, but remembering Polly's fears, she thought instantly of wild animals. Praying desperately that *someone* would come, she closed her eyes and counted to fifteen. When she opened them again, Seth Marple was standing across the tracks.

Seth, who had dark hair and eyes, was not very tall for his eleven years. He wore no shoes and no shirt, just overalls. He also was not what Emily called clean. In fact, Emily Upham had never seen anyone quite like him before, or certainly not so close.

"Hello," he said to her.

Emily turned away.

"Hello," Seth repeated.

Still Emily did not answer.

Seth stared at her for a full three minutes. "You dumb?" he finally inquired.

Emily replied without looking at him. "No," she said.

"Well, then," he asked, "what you doing?"

"Waiting."

"Who for?"

"My uncle."

Seth put his hands in his pockets and rocked on his heels. "Who's your uncle?" he asked.

"George P. Upham, banker at North Brookfield."

Seth was not sure he had heard correctly. "You say *North* Brookfield?"

Emily nodded.

Seth spoke carefully, taking his time. "Well, to tell the truth, there are a whole string of places with the name Brookfield on 'em around here. There's North Brookfield, just like you said. But there's also *East* Brookfield, and *West* Brookfield, and just *plain* Brookfield."

"My uncle lives in North Brookfield."

Seth considered this information by studying a loose spike in the railway bed. "This here banker," he said at last. "This Mr. Upham, the one who's supposed to meet you, you say he's your uncle?"

"Mama wrote a letter to him. She told him to meet me at the train."

"Did she?" said Seth, alarmed. "When was that?"

"Monday."

Seth began to feel queer, not at all certain what to say. He looked around to make sure no one was coming, then turned back to face Emily. "No," he finally said. "I'm not on speaking terms with any bankers."

"Could you find him?"

"Don't think I could," said Seth, not wanting to look at her.

"Oh," said Emily, disappointed. "Is a town far?"

"Few miles."

"Are they long miles?" asked Emily.

"Couldn't make 'em any longer if they tried."

"If you could take me there," Emily offered, "I would reward you."

Seth looked up with interest.

"I have no money," Emily explained quickly, "but my uncle would give you some."

Seth picked up some pebbles and threw them, one by one, into the bushes. "What's your name, anyway?" he asked as he threw the last pebble.

"Emily Octavia Upham."

"Nice meeting you," Seth said with a nod, then walked down the tracks, keeping his balance on one rail. A few yards along he stopped, sat down, and glanced back at the station hut. After five more minutes he walked back, balancing himself on the other rail.

"You figure to stay here all night?" he wanted to know.

"My uncle will come," Emily repeated, tears in her eyes.

Seth kicked at the railway ties with a heel. "Look here," he finally said. "I don't figure he will."

"Why?" asked Emily, her voice trembling.

"You say your ma wrote to him," began Seth. "Well, right there, that's no good. People hereabout don't get their mail regular. Mr. Marryat, the postmaster, he don't work half a lick. Always trying to get slaves and such to do the job. That's certain truth. And, like as not this uncle of yours never even got your ma's letter. That's possible. More than possible. Likely, even. Or maybe, maybe he can't even read. Some of the best folks 'round here can't read at all. And even after all that, I don't think you've got the right Brookfield. So, no, I don't think he'll come. You can best forget about that."

Emily, trying to follow all that Seth had been saying, felt her head start to ache.

"Whereabouts do you come from?" Seth asked.

"Boston."

"Well, you best go back quick as you can."

"How?" cried Emily.

"Beats me," Seth admitted.

Emily burst into tears.

Seth took a step into the hut, saying, "You're in a right bad way, aren't you?"

Emily slid away from him.

"You scared of me?" asked Seth, puzzled.

"Mama said not to talk to strangers," replied Emily in a whisper.

"Oh, shoot, I'm no stranger," said Seth. "Been around here for a long time. My name is —" Just in time he remembered it would be better if she did not know his name. "Anyway," he concluded, "you shouldn't stay here."

With a final nod, and thoroughly determined, Seth started down the tracks again. The sound of Emily's weeping made him stop. Disgusted, he made his way back, leaned on the hut, and looked down at her.

"I don't know what to do," said Emily in a small voice.

Seth walked to the back of the hut and studied a wasp nest that was being built underneath the roof. Then, his mind made up, he came back around to the front.

"Look here," said Seth. "I know of a place not so far away." He was thinking of his hideout. "You can go there."

"Is it a house?" Emily asked, rubbing the tears from her face with gloved fingers.

"Not exactly."

"With servants?"

"Nothing like that."

"With a bed for me to sleep on?" she tried.

"It's a place to sleep, all right," he told her. "Though it's not a regular bed."

Emily began to cry again.

"Now see here," Seth said, deciding he had to take drastic measures. "The fact is, you *have* to move. 'Cause you don't know the worst of it."

"What do you mean?" Emily asked between sobs.

"Hate to tell you," Seth confided in a low voice. "But you've gotten yourself into a country that has just about the worst thieves, bandits, and liars in the whole United States. *That's* the problem, and you might as well know it."

Emily's face became even paler than before. "What is your name?" she asked timidly.

Seth thought carefully before he spoke. "You

can call me Deadwood—Deadwood Dick."

"Deadwood Dick," repeated Emily. "I've never heard of such a name."

"Well, that's my name," he assured her solemnly. "This isn't Boston, is it?"

At the mere mention of Boston Emily had resumed her sobbing, tears streaming down her face. Her clothes were becoming more and more dirty. She was hungry. And it was getting on toward evening.

"See here," tried Seth. "I suppose you *could* stay. The truth is, though, there are bears and such 'round here this time of year. You might as well know that too."

Instantly Emily stopped crying. "Bears?" she asked in a voice that was mostly whisper but contained a fair part of fear.

"Well, sure," Seth informed her, feeling more and more anxious about getting her to move. "This is pretty much the West, ain't it?"

"I will go to your house," said Emily carefully, "if it is neat and clean and proper."

"It's proper all right," Seth assured her.

"Built it myself. But we better go." He started to walk off.

Her hesitation fading, Emily stood up, parasol in hand, and began to follow. Abruptly she stopped.

"Boy," she called.

"Deadwood," Seth corrected her.

"Please take my traveling bag."

Seth looked at her, then came back, picked up the bag, and started off, Emily once again following.

But again she stopped. "I have to have my trunk, too," she said.

Seth had forgotten about the enormous box still sitting on the road. "Can't," he announced. "Maybe tomorrow, but not now."

"I can't leave it," Emily pleaded. "I mustn't."

Seth, holding the small bag, looked from the girl to the trunk. "I suppose I could push it into the bushes," he suggested, not wanting her to cry again. "No one would find it."

Seth went over to the trunk, which loomed taller than he was. After a brief study he gave it a push. It wouldn't move.

"What you got in here?" he asked.

"My summer clothing."

"Whatever it is, I'm going to need your help to move it."

"I mustn't do that."

"Why not?"

"My gloves will get dirty."

"Take 'em off, then."

Emily closed her eyes.

"Now what you doing?" Seth wanted to know.

". . . three, four, five—I'm counting to fifteen —six, seven . . ."

"What the devil for?"

". . . eight, nine—it's not right to get excited —ten, eleven . . ."

Seth, now desperate to leave, jumped to the top of the trunk, swung his weight, and let the trunk crash over to the ground.

"Please be careful," said Emily, who was standing by, her parasol over her head.

Seth, ignoring her, squared his heels into the dirt and began to push against the trunk with his back.

It took an hour, but Seth managed to get the

trunk into the bushes. Once there, he hid it under branches and leaves.

"There!" he said when he was done. "Bandits won't find it now."

Seth moved out of the gully. "Just where are your ma and pa?" he asked as they went along.

"My mama is ill and with my aunt," said Emily. "Papa went to get money."

Seth stopped. "Get money?"

"He must have it," Emily tried to explain, not entirely sure why this was so. "And when he learns how kind you have been to me, he will give you some. We are rich," she added. "But I wish there was no money."

Seth eyed her with wonder. "Why not?"

"It makes people do and say wrong things," Emily insisted.

They came out on the main road. Seth, carrying the traveling bag, kept a few paces ahead of Emily, who despite the late hour, still had her parasol open. Out in the open, Seth became fearful that they might be seen. Stepping into the bushes at the side of the road, he started to go by another path. Emily, however, would not leave the main road.

"What's the matter now?" he asked.

"I would rather take the road," she said.

"You don't want us to be seen, do you?"

"I'll get dirty," said Emily shyly.

"Ain't no dirt in these bushes that I can see," said Seth.

But Emily would not move.

"All right," said Seth, giving in. "But you better follow close. If somebody does come along, don't worry about getting dirty or not, just keep out of sight."

Seth continued down the road. But Emily walked at a pace so slow that Seth found it painful. The more time they took, the more he worried that they would be discovered. Finally, when Emily wasn't looking, he picked up a rock and threw it against a tree. Emily jumped at the noise.

"What's that?" she cried.

"Oh," said Seth in an easy tone, "maybe a lion or some such. But you don't have to worry. Mostly they're friendly. They're only after the bears, not folks like us."

After that, Emily walked much faster.

But just before the turnoff to the hideout, Seth heard the clatter of a wagon and a loud voice singing. He didn't want to see who it was. "Bandits!" he cried. Without waiting for Emily to react, he pulled her into the bushes with him. Frightened, she offered no resistance.

Within moments the wagon rolled by. It was Preacher Farnlee and Banker Upham. The frowning, unhappy preacher was holding the reins. Mr. Upham, sporting a bottle, was singing in a loud voice. They passed by slowly.

"Were they bandits?" Emily asked.

"Were they!" cried Seth. "You don't know half the luck you just had. It was a good thing I found you. That was the *chief* bandit." With that he described Mr. Upham.

"I saw him *drinking*," said Emily with horror.

"Drinks all the time," Seth assured her. "And I'll tell you, if you ever see him again, you better run the other way fast as you can. He's famous for putting innocent folks where they don't want to be."

It was almost dark when they reached Seth's hideout. In fact, Emily didn't realize at first that they had reached it. When Seth told her, she was disappointed.

Seth's hideout consisted of a number of wooden boards propped up against four trees that had grown in a rough square. A hole in one of the boards served as a window, while the door was a cloth draped down over a gap between two of the boards. The roof was made up of two old doors.

"I thought it would be bigger," Emily said weakly.

"It's my home," Seth assured her. "Built it myself. It's got a window, too. Not with any glass, of course, but it's regular enough to look out."

"Where do you sleep?" Emily asked.

Seth drew back the cloth over the entry and pointed to a pile of hay in the far corner. "Pretty fresh, too. Got it just last month. Best thing about this place though, is nobody knows about it at all."

Emily remained motionless by the entrance.

"Now you don't *have* to stay here," Seth told her, seeing her hesitation. "You can sleep out in the woods. There's bears, like I told you. Or you

can take your pick of the Brookfields. That's bandits. You could climb a tree, too, I guess. That's
mostly snakes and such. But you're welcome to
stay here if you like."

Emily felt numb. Still she paused. "I must
know something," she whispered.

"Shoot," he told her.

"Are you a Christian?" she asked softly.

It was not the question Seth had expected.
"A Christian?" he repeated.

"Do you go to church?"

"I'll tell you," said Seth after a moment.
"The preacher and I were just having a talk today."

Emily felt better right away. "What were you
talking about?"

"He was pointing out some of the errors of
my ways and making some suggestions what to
do about them."

"Did you listen to him?" Emily asked.

"We both agreed I was in a tight spot," said
Seth. "We saw eye to eye about that."

"Then I will stay," Emily announced. Parasol and traveling bag in hand, she stepped inside.
It smelled damp and musty.

"You are very kind," whispered Emily. "My papa will reward you."

Seth touched his head in a salute. "Deadwood Dick does his duty," he said.

"And when my uncle comes, I'm sure he will give you what you deserve too."

Letting the cloth over the doorway drop, Seth went outside. Satisfied with the way things were going, he sat up against a tree. In the darkness it grew very quiet.

"Boy," Emily softly called.

"It's Deadwood," Seth reminded her. "And don't worry. I'm here. Not going anywhere."

"I'm hungry."

"We'll work 'round that in the morning," Seth told her. "You better get some sleep. I am."

"I have to say my prayers," she let him know.

"That's just fine," he told her. Then, curious, he crawled over by the door and listened.

"Bless papa," began Emily in a soft voice, "who went to find money. Forgive him for saying *that* word. Bless mama at her sister's house and help her get better. Bless my uncle, the banker, and help him find me soon. And bless this boy, who is the truest, most fearless and honest boy I

"Then I will stay," Emily announced.

have ever met, even though he is so awfully dirty."

In the darkness, Seth leaned back against the tree, thinking. Banker Upham, he reminded himself, had wanted to send him to some sort of boy's prison. It was both mean and unfair. But he had escaped, and now they thought he had gone for good. Didn't even know he was around at all. If they had known, they would have grabbed him and sent him off just as they promised. As far as Seth was concerned, he still had to get away.

Now Emily Upham, the banker's niece, had come. She was rich too, richest person he had ever met. What's more, she had promised that her father would give him lots of money if he got her back safely to Boston. The problem was, he would have to *get* money to get her back.

The only one around who had any money was banker Upham. Had heaps of it. Everyone knew that. He could spare some. And as far as Seth was concerned banker Upham was a thief, a real bandit. Seth could see no harm in taking money from a bandit.

Trouble was, Mr. Upham kept his money in

the bank. Still, as Seth knew from all his reading, banks were being robbed just about every other day. That would be something, he thought, robbing banker Upham's bank. It would take work, but he could do it. He *would* do it.

At that very moment Seth got his big idea: he would get Emily Upham to rob the bank. *That,* he decided, would be the best revenge.

He could even see how it would look as the title of a book: *Seth Marple's Revenge, or, How Deadwood Dick Saved the Banker's Niece. A Massachusetts Adventure.*

The next morning Emily slept late. Seth stayed as close to the hideout as possible, gathering and eating his fill of berries from nearby bushes. When he had eaten enough, he filled a tin pail with berries for Emily.

It was not until the middle of the morning that she awoke. At first she was puzzled, and then alarmed, about where she was. But as her sleepiness dropped away, she remembered all that had happened. By the time she was fully awake, she felt very hungry.

"Boy!" she called from inside the hut. "Boy!"

Seth scrambled to the entryway. "I'm here," he said. "And Deadwood Dick is my name."

"Is it time to get up?"

"Been up for hours."

"I'm very hungry."

Seth slid the pail of berries through the covered doorway. "Eat some and get yourself up. We've things to do."

Emily ate her fill. Then, after putting on a clean pinafore, she stepped out of the hut, parasol in hand.

"You're looking fine," he told her.

"Mama says that cleanliness is next to Godliness," Emily explained.

"Then your face is going to the Devil," Seth observed of her berry-stained face. But as soon as he had spoken he realized he had made a mistake.

"Please show me where you wash," said Emily, her voice trembling.

Seth, in fact, did little washing anywhere. But fortunately a creek was not far away, and he led the girl to it. After they reached it, he admired the care with which Emily washed.

"Don't you clean yourself?" Emily asked, seeing that Seth was only watching.

Embarrassed, Seth washed his face.

When he was done, Emily studied him. "You look much better when you wash your face, boy," she said. "It's the Christian thing to do. Even Polly says that."

On the way back to the hideout, Seth suddenly stopped. "Look here. There's just one thing. My name ain't 'Boy.' It's Deadwood Dick. You wouldn't want me to call you 'Girl,' would you?"

"You may call me Miss Emily."

3

THE BODY ON THE RAILS!

Back at the hideout, Seth told Emily to pay close attention to him. "Now," he began, "we have to get you back to Boston, don't we? That's what you want, isn't it?"

"Yes," Emily agreed. "To find mama."

"And your pa," Seth reminded her, the promised reward never far from his thoughts. "The point is," he continued, "we can't walk, can we? Or take a boat? Or borrow horses?"

Emily answered each question with a shake of her head.

"Well, then, that settles it out easy," he told her. "We've *got* to use the train. Excepting one thing. It takes money to use trains. So, we'll have to get money somewhere. Now, how much did it cost to get here from Boston?"

"I don't know," Emily replied. "Polly bought the ticket."

"Didn't you even see how much she spent?"

"I told you. I don't like money. Mama says that money is the root of all evil."

"Does she?"

Emily nodded.

Seth sat back, perplexed. "Well, we've still got to get it, and that means we've got to know how much to get. I guess *that's* what we have to find out first."

Emily shook her head. "No, there is something we must do before that," she said.

"What's that?"

Emily looked from Seth to his hideout. "Your house is not nice," she said.

"Why?" cried Seth, feeling hurt. "What's the matter with it? Suits me. And it doesn't leak, not much anyways."

Emily found it difficult to say what she meant. Going to the entryway, she looked in at the hut's emptiness. "It—" she began. "It should have a chair."

"What difference is a chair going to make?" cried Seth. "You can sit on a log, can't you? Sitting is sitting, far as I know."

"I must not stay unless it is nice," said Emily, her voice low.

"What if I can't find a chair?" Seth challenged.

Emily closed her eyes and counted to fifteen. "I will go to the bandits and beg for mercy," she said, sighing.

Seth stood up quickly. "Wouldn't want you to do that," he told her, truly alarmed. "I was just fooling. You stay here. I'll see what I can find."

Seth started off without a notion as to where he would find a chair. He knew of no chair in the woods, or any abandoned houses that might contain a chair, and the thought of going into town was out of the question. Nonetheless, he walked the main road, keeping to the edge in case anyone should come along.

This road led him to his mother's house. When he saw it, he stopped. He had quite forgotten all about his ma.

Seth was fond of his mother and knew she was fond of him, although he was aware that he caused her much heartache. As he stood looking at his home he worried that his leaving had caused his mother unhappiness. All the same, he did not want her to know that he was about. His whole plan depended upon people thinking he was gone. If his ma saw him, she would be certain to tell Mr. Farnlee.

Seth decided that the best plan would be to write her as soon as he reached Boston. For now, he went around the back of the house to avoid being seen. There he stopped short. Mr. Farnlee's wagon, mule still in harness, was standing at the back of the house. The preacher must have just arrived.

Wondering what the preacher *really* thought had happened to him, Seth decided to find out. The hole he had made at the back of the closet was as big and as open as he had left it. If he had come out that way, Seth reasoned, he could go back in the same fashion.

First, he peeked into the hole. It was dark, which meant that the closet door was closed. Quickly, and with as little sound as possible, Seth slipped inside. As soon as he was in the closet he heard Mr. Farnlee talking.

"He's not really a wicked boy, Mrs. Marple," the preacher was saying. "And you did all you could for him, so it is no fault of yours."

As his mother started to sob, Seth put his eye to a crack in the broken door. Mr. Farnlee, Bible in hand, was sitting next to Seth's mother.

"True," the preacher intoned, "he has gone to the wicked city of Albany. But it was not you who drove him there, Mrs. Marple, it was those wretched dime novels that were the cause. I grieve for you."

Mrs. Marple shook her head sadly. "He always seemed to get into trouble," she said.

"And not truly a bad boy," agreed Mr. Farnlee, "but a wayward one, nonetheless. Now he can no longer bring you the help and comfort you need. Fortunately," continued the preacher, drawing a deep breath, "there *are* those in the community who look to your welfare."

Mrs. Marple said nothing.

"Mrs. Marple," continued Mr. Farnlee with some difficulty, "if I may say so, I have a particular fondness for you."

"What," said Mrs. Marple after a moment's consideration, "what if Seth comes back?"

"Perhaps," said the preacher, "the Lord wished him to be gone. If he returns, he will only have to go to the workhouse. That is not of my doing. Mr. Upham is bound to it. Think of yourself," urged the preacher. "Think of me."

"I just keep wishing he's all right," Mrs. Marple said.

"Trust the Lord," urged Mr. Farnlee. "I offer you a new life."

"Perhaps Seth will turn up, Mr. Farnlee," said Mrs. Marple gently. "He would be your responsibility too."

"I would be the first to rejoice, Mrs. Marple, believe me. As his father, I might have a greater influence on him than I do now."

Mrs. Marple wistfully shook her head. "I do wish he would come home."

"Mrs. Marple," tried the preacher, "let us pray for guidance." So saying, he slipped down on his knees, placing his Bible on a stool that stood before him. "Will you join me?"

Mrs. Marple knelt by his side.

"Let us," the preacher's voice rang out, "ask for some *sign* from above!"

Turning their faces heavenward, both closed their eyes. The preacher began a prayer.

Seth had heard that prayer before and recognized it as a long one, all about signs and omens, the preacher asking for something to suggest that their prayers were not in vain. As the prayer continued, Seth carefully opened the closet door, reached out, and took the preacher's Bible. He put it in the closet. Seeing how easy it was, he reached out a second time and took the stool too.

Mr. Farnlee and Mrs. Marple, eyes closed, continued to pray. The preacher called for a sign, no matter how small. Mrs. Marple sighed, "Amen." Neither one noticed Seth.

Concluding his prayer, the preacher opened his eyes and reached for his Bible. It was not there. He looked around but was unable to find it. He stood up and hastily scanned the room, his face expressing fixed amazement.

Seth decided that it was time for him to leave.

"Mrs. Marple," whispered the preacher in a

voice that suggested a cork had caught in his throat, "Mrs. Marple, where did I place my Bible?"

Mrs. Marple opened her eyes. "Why, Mr. Farnlee, you placed it right over—" Her voice faded.

Silently, Seth slipped through the closet hole, taking with him both Bible and stool. Running as fast as he could, he hoped his gifts would bring pleasure to Emily.

As it turned out, a stool was not exactly what Emily had in mind. But when Seth related how he had to sneak into a nest of bandits to get it, she was properly impressed. She was even more delighted with his gift of the Bible, bestowing upon him a smile that made him feel uncomfortable.

"You are a gentleman, boy," she told him, hugging the book to her chest. Then she had a further thought. "But do these bandits read the Bible?"

"Not usually," said Seth, trying to find an answer. "Mostly it's just to look at the pictures."

The stool was only the beginning. Emily insisted on turning Seth's hideout into a Boston sitting room.

"It ain't worth the trouble," Seth protested. "We'll be in Boston in a few days, won't we?"

Emily would not be distracted. "Mama says we must always show by high example."

In point of fact Emily did not exactly *show* Seth. It was more that she talked, while he did the doing. First he cleaned the floor, then he fetched new straw. After that, the stool was set up. The Bible, opened to a nice page, was carefully placed upon it.

Having done all that, Emily opened her traveling bag and took out her special things. Seth was fascinated. She removed her pearl-handled comb and brush set. A necklace. A package of scented soap. A few dresses and a bright pinafore. Another pair of gloves. Finally, she brought out a framed photograph of her mother and father.

Seth studied the picture with intense interest. It was Emily's father's face that he examined with the greatest care, since he was the one who was going to reward Seth for saving Emily. Seth studied his face for signs of generosity.

Emily's father's resemblance to his brother, banker Upham, was not great. Whereas Mr. Upham was fully bearded like President Grant, Emily's father had only a mustache. Seth could see why Emily had not recognized her uncle on the road the day before.

When Emily had arranged things to her satisfaction, she informed Seth that there were things in her trunk that she needed. That was fine with Seth. He had already decided that the best way, the only way, to determine the fare to Boston was to stop a train and ask. That way, they would not have to go into town.

Seth led the way. Emily followed, her parasol shielding her from the sun.

They reached the tracks without incident. Seth cleared the hidden trunk of its leaves and branches, then Emily showed him how to unlatch it.

The trunk, to Seth's amazement, contained nothing but clothes. Seth didn't think that the North Brookfield General Store contained so many clothes. He looked at it all in wonder.

Seth studied his face for signs of generosity.

"You have anything red in there?" he asked.

"What for?"

"We have to stop the train, don't we? Everybody knows you can't stop trains without something red." He could see she did not understand.

"We have to know the fare, don't we?" he explained. "Best place to ask is the train. We can hide in the bushes and wait for one. 'Course, I'll have to listen to the whistles to make sure the train isn't planning to stop. When I'm sure it isn't, I'll wave something red. The train'll stop fast enough, and then we can ask."

Emily nodded. After removing a few pairs of shoes and some dresses, she produced a red shawl.

"That's the thing," he told her. "Now, let's go hide."

"Why do we have to hide?"

"Why, can't you see?" cried Seth, exasperated with her questions. "This is a bandit town, isn't it?"

Emily nodded.

"Well, then, who comes to bandit towns? Bandits, that's who. And who meets bandits? *Other* bandits. What we have to do is make sure none of 'em sees us."

Seth chose a spot among the bushes in the gully that was both safe and shady. There they waited. Within an hour they heard a train's first approaching whistle.

"Now be quiet," he warned Emily. "I've got to listen."

Seth concentrated on the whistles, which grew louder as the train drew closer. Soon he was able to determine that the train was not going to stop in North Brookfield. That learned, he looked out at the station road to see if anyone from town was there to hail the train. No one.

"Good enough," he told Emily, as the train drew closer. "Stay near me."

The train swung into the far end of the gully. Seth, holding the red shawl, ran down the tracks and began waving frantically. Emily, parasol over her head, stood apart, watching.

The train raced down the tracks, clanging its bell, blowing off steam, only to run right past where Seth was standing. The engineer waved in friendly fashion, as did some of the passengers, but the train did not even slow down.

Disgusted, Seth watched it go until it was out of sight.

"They were very friendly," said Emily, wishing silently that she had been on the train.

Seth stared down the empty tracks for a long time. "Well," he finally announced. "There's only one way to make a train stop."

"What is that?"

"If you were to lie down on the tracks, seeing as how you're a lady, a young lady anyways, they would stop sure enough. And when they did stop, I could ask them about the fare."

Emily's pale face became chalky white. "They might not stop," she said, her voice barely a whisper.

"Shoot," Seth assured her. "They always do. Best brakes in the whole United States!"

"My dress will get dirty," suggested Emily, her voice trembling.

"Oh, you've got so many dresses, you could lie on the tracks every time a train came by, and it wouldn't matter."

Emily counted to fifteen. "I do not think my mama would like it," she cried.

Seth attempted to argue, but Emily only closed her eyes and shook her head wildly. When tears began to roll down her face, Seth was finally moved to try to think of another way.

"Look here," he said at last. "As I figure it, maybe you're right. It's not so much *you* they would be stopping for, anyway. It's your fancy clothes. Now, since you've got so many of 'em, what we could do is stuff one of 'em up, make it *look* like it was you, and put *that* on the tracks."

Emily, relieved that she would not have to lie down on the tracks before an oncoming train, agreed to Seth's new idea faster than she might otherwise have done. Seth hurried over to the trunk and opened it.

"Pick a real fancy one," he instructed her.

Emily, unable to come to a decision, took a long time.

"It's you or the dress," Seth warned.

Reluctantly Emily made her choice. But once she gave the dress to Seth, he demanded shoes and stockings. Mournfully, she complied.

When he had all that he needed, Seth busied himself with gathering weeds and leaves to stuff the dress. When he had done it, it looked like a scarecrow, a child scarecrow to be sure, but Seth thought it looked good enough. Not long after he had finished they heard a train whistle.

"Into the bushes," he warned her.

They hid as they had done before, first making certain that the train was neither planning to stop nor that anyone from North Brookfield was getting on board.

As soon as he was sure that they would not be observed, Seth, lugging the stuffed dress, ran to the side of the tracks. Emily, under orders, carried the red shawl.

Into the gully the train swung, its plume of smoke pulsing from its huge bell stack, steam leaking from every valve. When the train was in full view, Seth heaved the stuffed dress over the rails. It landed perfectly upon the tracks, its bulging stockings flopping mournfully over the ties.

"Wave the shawl," Seth yelled to Emily.

Emily did as she was told.

The locking brakes squealed like two dozen hogs stuffed into a cigar box; the sound could be heard for miles. Steam blew out of every hole. Cars slammed into one another. The engine wheels, locked and no longer turning, slid over the rails and made the sparks fly like the Fourth of July. Two inches from the stuffed dress, the train came to a dead halt.

People poured out of the cars, shouting and yelling, some holding bloody noses. "What's happened? Anyone killed?"

Emily, frightened, fled to the protection of the bushes. But Seth remained where he was.

The conductor rushed up. "Clear the way!" he cried. "Who's lying there? Stand back. Who is that?"

"Ain't nobody," Seth told them. "Nothing but clothes. I just wanted to know how much the fare is to Boston."

The conductor and the engineer looked at Seth. Then they looked again at the stuffed clothing laying on the tracks.

"It would cost *you* a flat hundred dollars," snapped the conductor, "and you still might not get there!" Turning about, he herded the passengers back on the train.

After the train had gone, Emily came out of the bushes where she was hiding. "They were very, very angry, weren't they?" she asked.

Seth covered the trunk with branches and leaves. "That's the way people always are to me," he told her cheerfully.

Once the trunk was hidden again, Seth led

Emily back toward the hideout. A hundred dollars seemed an awful lot of money just to get to Boston, but at least now he knew how much they needed to get from the bank.

4

MYSTERIOUS STRANGER!

While Seth and Emily were making their way back to the hideout, Mr. Upham was sitting in the largest room of his house. His house was the biggest in North Brookfield and was placed on Thistle Hill, the highest point in town. Set behind massive elms, the house looked out over the valleys, giving the banker a sense of power over all he surveyed.

At the moment, however, banker Upham felt no power at all. Sitting across from him in partial darkness was a man who kept his face purposefully within the shadows.

The two men had been talking in low, angry

tones. The stranger had spoken his piece with direct simplicity, outlining exactly what he wanted. It was time for Mr. Upham to reply.

"I tell you I can't give you that much money," said Mr. Upham, slapping his black accounts box, which was, as always, by his side.

"Then I'll expose you," came the cool reply.

"That won't do," sighed the banker. "It won't do at all."

"I'll do it for certain," said the man. "Only too happy to do it. You may bang your black box all you want, it won't help with me."

"What," asked the banker in a tone he did not often take, "will you make public?"

The stranger sat back in his chair. "I suppose the good people of North Brookfield would like to know what you did with the tax money deposited in your bank."

"They will get the money back, every cent!"

"What if they want it right now, as is their privilege?" the man asked.

Mr. Upham remained silent.

"Then," continued the stranger, "there is the little matter of building a railway spur directly into town. And yes, the new station that has been suggested. I understand that the Road Committee, which you have the honor of leading, has chosen the best route and the best builder."

"What about it?" demanded the banker, scowling.

"The land that *your* committee proposes as the best, as the only route possible, is owned by Consolidated Land Limited. The construction company chosen is the Massachusetts Building Company."

"Nothing wrong there," protested the banker.

"George P. Upham is a principal stockholder in both companies," said the man.

The banker said nothing.

"Do you wish me to go on?" asked the stranger. "I can."

Mr. Upham conceded. "It's not necessary."

"I need four thousand dollars," came the demand.

"I told you, I simply cannot spare it," protested Mr. Upham. "I would be bankrupt. If you know so much about my affairs, you should know that too."

"I need four thousand dollars," came the demand.

The stranger thought a moment. "Is your bank insured?"

"Of course."

"Why then," suggested the man, "I'll *rob* your bank of four thousand dollars. That way I shall have the money I need, and you shall get it all back from the insurance company."

"There's not that much money *in* the bank!" cried Mr. Upham.

"Put it in," said the stranger, coldly. "That should not be too difficult."

"It's Saturday," Mr. Upham objected. "The bank is closed. If I went into town and then to the bank, people would notice and might remember."

"Do it at night when nobody is about," suggested the man.

The banker considered this for a long time. "I shall do it on one condition," he said. When the stranger did not reply, he went on. "You have got to make the robbery look big. It musn't look as if you just walked into the safe and plucked up what you wanted."

"I'll blow up the safe," said the man.

"That will cost me more money!" cried Mr. Upham.

The stranger leaned forward. "Look here, Mr. George P. Upham," he said, his voice full of scorn. "I will have that money."

"Very well," said the banker nervously. "But you must not remain here. Someone will see you. I'll tell you a safe place in the woods where you can go."

"Very good," agreed the stranger, getting to his feet. "I'm only too happy to do what will be most comfortable for you. You put the money in tonight. I shall take it out tomorrow."

5

DISCOVERY!

Emily took her time setting out the things that she had brought back from the trunk. Seth spent most of his afternoon collecting food. On the whole, he had the more successful venture. When he got back, Emily was still not satisfied with the placement of her shoes.

"Didn't we agree to take the train to Boston?" he asked her.

"Yes," she agreed.

"Why, from that stretch of shoes there, it looks to me like you aim to walk to Boston on regular schedule."

"They are for different times," Emily explained, giving the particulars of each pair.

Seth, who wore no shoes, listened with disbelief. But he showed Emily the collection of food he had made—early corn, some vegetables, and a chicken that he said he had borrowed. He offered them all to Emily.

Emily informed him that she knew nothing whatever about cooking.

"You don't eat this kind of stuff *raw,* do you?" Seth asked, horrified.

"Susan is the cook," said Emily. "And Polly serves. It's Katherine who does the washing up."

Seth felt sorry for her. "That doesn't leave much for you to do, does it? What do you do with all your time?"

"You won't understand," cried Emily in vexation. "I'm a lady! Ladies don't *do* anything."

"They eat, don't they?" insisted Seth.

There was no choice to it. Seth got the food together while Emily watched. First he plucked the chicken. Then, after much rubbing and blowing, he got a fire going. Taking up the tin pail he filled it part way with water, threw in the food, and put the entire mixture up to boil.

To Emily's surprise, it tasted good.

After they ate, Seth decided to explain the next step of his plan.

"That conductor," he began, "said it took a hundred dollars to get to Boston. That's just one of us. And you'll need me to go along. That's two hundred dollars that we have to get."

Emily nodded solemnly.

"Well, I've got an idea where that money might be," Seth blurted out.

"Where?"

"Like I told you before, this is bandit country. Well, all the bandits, from all over, take all the money they've stolen and put it in this one place. What I suggest is that we go get some of that."

"That would be stealing," said Emily, shocked.

"They stole it first, didn't they?" said Seth. "Anyway, we're just taking it back. Fair's fair, as I see it. The whole thing is," Seth hurried on to say, not wanting to discuss that point too closely, "we *have* to get that money, else we'll be staying here for a hundred years or such."

Emily sighed. Looking up at the darkening sky, she felt chilly.

"Now," continued Seth, when Emily said

nothing. "Won't be any danger to it. Not a speck. It'll be easy. The point is, I'm going to make sure of that. Here's my plan. When you go to sleep, I'll scout out the bandit's camp and make a plan to get some of that stolen money."

"They will catch you," Emily whispered.

"Won't," Seth assured her. "Not a chance."

"I don't want to be alone," she said.

"You won't even notice. You'll be asleep."

"I'll wake."

"Just don't, that's all."

"I will," she insisted, pulling at her sleeve.

"I won't go an inch till you're asleep, and I'll be back before you wake."

Without saying anything else, Emily went into the hideout. There she slowly prepared herself for sleeping. First she read her new Bible, then she recited her prayers. Seth had never been so blessed in all his life.

"Good night," Emily called.

"Good night," Seth answered, sitting up against the hut. Soon it was completely dark. The moon began to rise. A few embers in the fire winked and glowed. Seth listened. Not a sound. Slowly, carefully, he began to get up.

"Boy!" cried Emily.

Seth slumped back down. "I'm here," he called and resigned himself to wait some more. When he was sure she was finally asleep, he again rose.

"Boy! Did you go yet?" she called.

"If you don't stop calling me 'Boy,' I'll leave you whether you're asleep or not, you hear?"

"I'm sorry," said Emily, her voice quivering. "Do you forgive me?"

"I'm trying."

"Please."

"Okay, I forgive you."

The moon was high. The fire embers had burned themselves out. The sound of an owl filled the air. Carefully, Seth got up. He paused. This time Emily didn't call.

Moving silently and cautiously until he was far from the hideout, Seth soon reached the main road. The moonlight provided enough light for him to go quickly, though he clung to the edge of the road just in case someone else was abroad.

In a short time he reached North Brookfield.

The town of North Brookfield was not large.

It contained little more than the main street that ran down its middle. The few side streets were hardly bigger than paths. Homes intermixed with stores lined the way. There was a post office, a general store, a meeting house, Mr. Farnlee's church, and a few public buildings. And in the very center of the town was the bank. Mr. Upham's bank.

It was the only bank in town. Not counting the church, with its spire, the bank was the largest building, one of the few buildings that Seth had never entered. Standing next to the town hall, it was built of brick, with two white wooden columns that held up an extended roof high over the doorway. It was considered quite the grandest building in the area.

Carefully Seth worked his way down the main street, moving with ever greater caution, pausing to listen at the slightest sound. Nothing disturbed him but a barking dog, and even the dog soon stopped.

When Seth reached the bank, the twin columns flanking the double doors looked like guards. A quick tug told him that the doors were shut tightly.

Recollecting a back door, Seth decided to go down a narrow alley that ran alongside the bank. This he did with ease. He was, in fact, just about to step around the corner of the building to the back door when he saw someone coming. Soundlessly, Seth dropped to the ground where he stood, then poked his head around the corner to take a look.

Whoever it was, was coming directly toward the bank, carrying a large object in one hand. As he watched, Seth saw the person go to the same door that he had hoped to enter, jiggle the lock, pull out some keys, unlock the door, pull the door open, step into the building, and disappear from view. The door shut again.

Slowly Seth came to his feet. Something about the form of the person—a man—seemed familiar, but he couldn't quite place him. He had the feeling that if he could see the man's face, he would recognize him instantly. He crept closer to the door to try to get a glimpse of the man inside the bank.

As he stood there, Seth was stricken with a sudden fear; whoever was inside, was robbing the bank, and there might not be enough money left for him and Emily to go to Boston. It was a terrible thought. It made him angry to think about it. He had to do something.

At the door, he put his ear to the crack. It did not reveal a thing. Cautiously, he gave the door-knob a twist and a slight pull. The door opened noiselessly. He waited to see what would happen. Nothing did. Encouraged, he pulled the door shut behind him.

It was very dark inside the bank, much darker than outside. With his hands in front of him, Seth felt his way, inching forward, trying to adjust his eyes to what light there was. Then, up ahead, he saw a faint glow of light.

Dim though the light was, Seth was able to make out where he was. He was in a big room with a number of desks and chairs. Opposite was a wall with more doors, one of which was open. The light was coming through that open door. Careful as ever, Seth crept forward.

He heard sounds, but could not decide what they were. Reaching the door, he peeked into the room. The man was kneeling on the floor, his back toward Seth. By the man's side was a hooded lantern, its light shining toward a large metal safe. And the safe door had been swung open.

Seth's heart gave a leap. His worst fears were being realized. The bank was being robbed.

But as he watched he realized that it was not an ordinary bank robbery. The man at the safe was not taking money *out* of the safe, he was putting money *in* the safe.

Seth was puzzled. He had read a great deal about robbing banks, but the only way he had ever read of its being done was by taking money *out*. Whoever he was watching was shoveling money into the safe by the fistful.

The man had finished. He silently swung the safe door shut, his keys jangling as he locked it. Seth took three quick steps across the room to one of the desks. Going behind it, he dropped to his knees and peered out.

The man turned away from the safe and toward Seth. Instantly Seth recognized him. It was George P. Upham, the banker, Emily's uncle. Seth could see now that it was his black box that he was carrying.

Lantern in hand, Mr. Upham looked around the room. He put the box on the floor and walked up to a wall on which hung a portrait of George Washington. He took the picture down, revealing a hole in the wall. There he deposited his keys, returned the picture to the wall, and gathered up his black box.

After a final look around the room, Mr. Upham went out of the building. Seth could hear the door shut, the lock snap.

Seth just sat there, not understanding anything about what had happened. He told himself that he didn't know very much about the banking business. Perhaps this was the way that things were done.

Still, he wanted to check what was in the safe. There would be no point in robbing it if there was not enough to pay their fares to Boston. It had surely looked like a lot of money that Mr. Upham was stuffing into the safe; he wanted to be sure.

Seth's eyes were now accustomed to the darkness. He slid back the picture of George Washington, reached into the hole, and took out the keys. He needed only a few minutes at the safe to fit the proper key. The door swung open.

He took the picture down, revealing a hole in the wall.

Inside were shelves and boxes. But on top of everything was a pile of money, more money than he had ever seen in his whole life—hundreds and hundreds of dollars. Seth put his hands into the pile just to get the feel of it.

Satisfied that there was enough money for their trip, he withdrew his hands and started to swing back the door. Then he stopped. He pulled the door open again.

Seth stared at the money, knowing that he could take it right then. No, he decided, if *he* took it, it would be regular stealing. If *Emily* took it, why that would be a real revenge. It would make it almost honest. Quickly, so as not to be tempted further, he swung the safe door shut and locked it.

With a clear conscience, Seth returned the keys to the hole in the wall. Knowing that the back door was locked, he climbed on a desk, slid the window open above it, and crawled out.

He hurried back to the hideout. Emily was still sleeping.

In moments, Seth was sleeping too.

6

GREAT BANK ROBBERY!

The next morning was Seth's turn to sleep late. Emily's voice woke him.

"Boy!" she called out.

Seth, struggling through his sleep, tried to ignore her.

"Boy!" she repeated.

"What do you want?"

"I'm hungry."

Seth rolled over to shield his eyes from the morning sun but made no answer.

"Won't you get some food for me?" asked Emily.

Seth felt annoyed. "Why don't you get it for yourself?"

Emily considered this. "I don't know how."

"The fact is," suggested Seth, propping his arms beneath his head, "you're just lazy."

"I'm not."

"Why, you expect me to do everything for you, don't you?"

"I'm a young lady," said Emily, mournfully.

"Look here," continued Seth. "Last night I snuck into the bandits' camp. There must have been a hundred of them, all with guns and looking mean and stuff, just itching to catch me, skin me, murder me, and all that. Even the bandit chief was there. You saw him. He's the meanest man around.

"And all that while you were sleeping like a kernel of corn on a cob. Now, I'm only doing this for you. Don't you want to go back to Boston? Don't you want to see your ma and pa?"

Emily pulled back the curtain of the door and looked at Seth, stretched out on the ground. "I do," she said.

Seth sat up. "Well, it's not going to be easy, is it? I'm not going to be able to do it all by myself anymore. We need the money from the bandit chief to go back to Boston. Don't you think you could help me just a little bit?"

"I don't know how," said Emily softly. "I just don't." Her voice shook a little.

"I'm willing to teach you if you're willing to learn," Seth said.

Emily ran back into the hut, quickly put on a new dress, and came out ready to help with breakfast.

Seth looked at her. Aside from the clean dress, she was, by his lights, looking more human every day. Her hair was unkempt, her hands and face weren't the awful white they were when he first met her, her stockings hung limp, and her shoes were scuffed.

Feeling he was making progress, Seth led Emily to the blackberry patch. The girl did try, but she cried about pricking her fingers on thorns and cried even more when she wiped her juice-stained fingers on her white clothing, which caused a stain like a ghastly scar.

But, after a while, she got used to it. Seth allowed her plenty of times to rest, and she almost came to enjoy what she was doing. When Seth led her to some farms to gather vegetables, she made no protest at all. Altogether, Seth was pleased with her education.

They had an easy day. Seth made certain not to mention that they were going to get the money that very night. He wanted Emily to relax and not to worry. He knew that he could teach her only a little bit at a time. Toward evening, after they had eaten their fill, Seth decided to bring up *the* subject.

"Tell you what," he began, as if the thought had just occurred to him. "Suppose we get that money tonight."

Instantly Emily stopped her game of piling sticks over leaves. "Now?" she said, her voice full of alarm.

"When it's dark, leastways."

"I'll be scared."

"Nothing to it," he assured her. "Asides, I'll be with you."

Emily resumed stacking sticks. "What if they catch us?" she asked.

"Won't," said Seth easily. "Just won't. Wouldn't dare to. I worked it all out so there's not even one chance in the whole world of that."

"But what if they *do*," Emily insisted.

"Look here," replied Seth, annoyed at her challenge. "I tell you they won't. Anyway, if we don't get the money, you'll be here forever. I don't suppose you want that, do you? Don't you want to be in Boston by tomorrow?"

"I guess so," said Emily.

"All right, then, we're agreed. When it gets good and dark, we'll go. You'll see, we won't be taking any chance at all. You can even get some sleep. I'll wake you when it's time."

Emily pushed away her sticks and stared at her hands. "I don't think I can sleep," she said quietly.

Seth flung himself down on the ground, hands beneath his head. "Better rest up, any-ways."

Emily retreated into the hideout. But she had been right; far too nervous, she lay down, her eyes open, staring at the ceiling made of doors. Finally she got up and went outside. "I just can't sleep," she told Seth. "I can't."

"I guess that's all right," said Seth, stirring up the fire a bit so it wouldn't seem so dark.

Emily stared at the hot coals. "If I could, I would burn up all money."

"Burn money?" cried Seth. "Why would you do that?"

"It makes people do the wrong thing." When Seth didn't answer, she continued cautiously. "Sometimes, sometimes I think you don't always tell the truth."

"Oh, shoot, I do. Always. Swear it," insisted Seth, feeling bad.

"It is wrong to tell lies, isn't it?" she asked.

"And that's just why I don't tell none," agreed Seth.

Emily looked at the glowing fire again, not sure whether the embers made her feel better or not. They reminded her of Hell. "I know a poem about lies," she announced.

"Let's hear it."

Automatically Emily stood, clasped her hands in front of her, and began, "Don't tell a lie."

> *Don't tell a lie, dear children,*
> *No matter what you do.*
> *Own up and be a hero,*
> *Right honest, brave and true.*

> *The rod but hurts your body,*
> > *While lies deform your soul.*
> *Don't mind the present smarting,*
> > *Keep your spirit pure and whole.*

Emily curtsied and sat down.

Seth was beginning to feel more and more uncomfortable. "That's real nice," he told her.

"I believe it," she said with the utmost seriousness.

Seth thought about it for a moment. "Your pa ever take the rod to you?" he wanted to know.

"Oh, no!" she cried. "He *wouldn't*. I *never* tell lies!"

"Well," said Seth, "I'll be straight with you. I've tried 'em both, rod and lies. It's not like your poem says at all. I mean, it's a pretty poem and such, and you spoke it good, but the rod hurts a whole lot more. A whole lot."

Emily said nothing.

Emily had not said a word since she had recited her poem. Seth, too, had remained silent, feeling more and more nervous, not for himself, but for her. It seemed to him that the night was darker than it had been the night before.

"Don't tell a lie dear children / No matter what you do."

Unable to wait any longer, he got up. "It's time," he whispered.

Emily, kneeling before the fire, began to sob.

"You can't always go crying," he told her sharply.

"They'll catch me," she said.

"Won't!" he insisted. "No chance at all." When Emily still did not move, he decided to threaten her. "Now you can come or I'm just going to go myself. I'll get the money and go to Boston without you if I have to. I'll find your ma. I'll tell her you didn't even *try* to come home. You can stay here if you want." He turned to go.

Emily jumped up. "Wait!"

Seth paused.

"I'll go," she said.

Emily stumbled so much, crying out each second, that Seth had to take her hand and lead the way until they reached the main road. Seth wasn't sure what time it was when they got there. He figured it was close to midnight. There was not a sound anywhere. On the open road there was enough moonlight for them to see the road clearly.

Emily felt better for the easier passage and

stopped asking if there were bandits behind each tree, though she did refuse to let go of Seth's hand.

They passed Seth's home without pausing and soon reached the outskirts of town. There Seth stopped.

"Now see here," he whispered. "It'll look like a town. It is a town, but it's a bandit town, sure enough."

Emily looked down the empty main street. "Do you think my uncle lives here?" she suddenly asked.

"I told you, told you a million times, he doesn't!" cried Seth. "I can't go over all that again. Ain't no one here around even like that. Why, wouldn't he have gotten that letter if he did live here?"

Emily, under his anger, hung her head. "I guess so."

"Now pay attention to what we're going to do and just do it."

Seth led her around by the back of the town houses. Emily, as much afraid of a scolding by Seth as by anything else, dared not say a word. They reached the back of the bank easily.

"This is it," Seth whispered.

"I never knew bandits lived in town," said Emily. "They all looked like regular houses."

"That's the way they are, exactly, always tricking folks," explained Seth. "Now, we have to go through the back door."

"Are we allowed to?" asked Emily.

"Course we are," Seth insisted. "They're thieves, aren't they? And I just wish you wouldn't keep asking the same things all the time. Come on!"

With Emily in tow Seth moved up to the back door. There he tried the door handle, pulled it, but it was locked up shut. He had forgotten that Mr. Upham had opened the door for him the night before.

Emily saw his hesitation. "What's the matter?" she asked, instantly alarmed.

"You see," he said. "The door's locked. They don't trust anybody."

He led the way along the side alley. "We'll have to try this," he said, coming to a stop under the window.

Emily kept looking about nervously, staying close to Seth.

He tried the window, which came up easily. "There, you see," he pointed out, "nothing to it."

With a quick jump, Seth hoisted himself up to the window. Leaning inside, he first took a look around. Nothing was there to discourage him. Pulling himself up the rest of the way, he leaned through the window and slipped down on the desk below. He turned around and leaned out for Emily.

"Come on," he called, holding his arms out to her.

"I can't!" she cried.

"Have to!" he shouted in a whisper.

Trembling, Emily lifted her arms. Seth grabbed her by her wrists and pulled. Kicking and struggling, she banged her way up against the brick sides of the bank so loudly that Seth was certain she would bring somebody out to check the bank. He pulled harder. When her dress ripped, Emily squealed. She was so frightened when she got inside the bank that she was shaking.

"You'd think you never went in through a window before," Seth scolded.

"I never did," answered Emily, her voice caught in surpressed sobs.

In the moonlight Seth saw her shut her eyes and start counting. He pulled at her. "Come on. We've got to get the money." He jumped down from the desk. Enough light came in so that he could see the picture of George Washington on the wall. He went right to it and started to take it down.

"You mustn't!" cried Emily.

Seth jumped around. "I mustn't what?"

"That's George Washington," said Emily. "He *never* told a lie!"

"Don't be a fool," returned Seth, taking down the picture. Reaching into the hole behind it, he pulled out the keys. He started to leave the picture where it was, but under Emily's reproachful gaze he put it back.

With the keys in one hand, and holding Emily with the other, he turned to the safe.

Then everything started to happen.

Except for their own steps and an occasional bump into a desk, everything had been quiet. But as Seth turned toward the safe, the sound of a galloping horse could be heard. Seth became motionless, straining to hear.

"What is it?" said Emily, sensing his alarm.

"Somebody," said Seth, still listening.

Emily's voice went higher with each word she spoke. "Are they coming here?"

Again Seth listened to the galloping. "No, I don't think so."

Even as he spoke he was proved wrong. The hoofbeats stopped right in front of the bank. They heard a thud, then a tremendous crash at the front of the building.

Emily started to scream, but Seth swung around and clapped his hand over her mouth, dragging her back toward a desk. Willingly, she dove with him under the nearest one.

"It's bandits!" she cried. "They'll catch us."

Seth was not sure what was happening. Not that he had much time to think about it. Someone came stamping down toward the room they were in. Oblivious to the noise he was making, the man held a lantern before him so that he could see where he was going. He was, in fact, going to the same spot where Seth and Emily were.

Behind the desk, Emily knelt on the floor, her

hands covering her face. Seth was afraid to look and afraid not to look. He chose to look; it was only one person.

But that one person was enough. The man seemed enormous and was made even more frightening by the bandanna that he had tied around his face. And while in one hand he held a lantern, his other hand held a bag and a revolver.

The man stood still for a moment, swinging the lantern about. When he saw the room where the safe was, he ran into it.

Seth could now see nothing. He could only hear sounds of tinkering and fussing. In seconds, the man came out of the safe room, only to be followed by an awful explosion. Papers flew all around them. Chairs fell over. The picture of George Washington crashed down. The air was filled with dust.

Through the dust, the thief leaped back into the safe room. Seth dared another look. The man was crouching in front of the safe, pulling out the money and stuffing it into his bag. When he came out the second time, his bandanna had slipped from his face. Seth recognized him at once. He had seen his picture: it was Emily's pa.

7

IN PURSUIT!

When Seth saw that the robber was Emily's father, he was more stunned by the revelation than he had been by the explosion. He was, in fact, horrified.

Emily, far under the desk, her eyes closed, had not seen her father. Having reached one thousand, she was still counting.

Emily's father had taken but a minute to rush out of the bank. Once he was gone Seth made his way through the smoke to the room where the safe still sat. The door was bent and useless. Worse, the safe was empty. The money that Mr. Upham had put into the safe the night before was gone. Not a penny was left. Emily's father had taken everything.

Seth was still standing in front of the safe trying to understand what had happened when shouting made him realize that he and Emily were in great danger. The townspeople were gathering at the front of the bank.

Regaining his sense of urgency, Seth flung down the keys he still held and ran out of the safe room. He and Emily had to get away as quickly as possible. He found her beneath the desk, her hands still covering her eyes.

"Come out!" he shouted. "Bandits!"

"Are they going to catch us?"

"We can get out of here before they do," he told her, pulling at her arm.

But Emily refused to budge. Instead she closed her eyes and once more began to count.

"Count all you want later," Seth yelled. Dragging her by her hand, Seth moved toward the window through which they had entered. The shouting at the front of the bank was growing louder.

"What's happened?" cried one voice.

"Bank robbery!" shouted another.

"They still in there?" asked a third.

"Get your guns and let's get 'em!" yelled a fourth.

Seth climbed to the top of the desk beneath the window, hauling Emily up after him.

"What will they do to us?" she kept asking.

"If we get out, nothing," Seth replied.

Emily slipped down on her knees and began to pray. "Oh," she sobbed, "why did Papa ever say *that* word!"

Seth poked his head out the window and looked up and down the alley. A mob of people with torches were by the front door of the bank. Some, he saw, had guns. Momentarily he wondered if they had caught Emily's pa.

"Now," he whispered urgently, pulling Emily back to her feet again. "I'll go first, then you jump. That's all you have to do. I'll catch you easy enough."

"I can't!" she cried.

"Have to."

The noise of the crowd now began to come from inside the bank. "They must still be in there!" someone shouted. Once more came the call, "Bring up the guns!"

Seth dared not wait any longer. He leaned out the window head first, then kicked.

"Come out with your hands up!" came a command from outside the office where Seth and Emily were.

Out the window Seth went, tumbling down on his back with a thump. Just as quickly, he leaped to his feet and called to Emily. "Come on, jump!"

Emily stuck her frightened face out the window. "They're coming in!" she cried.

"I'll catch you," Seth pleaded.

"They're coming, they're coming!" she screamed.

"Jump!" Seth yelled for the last time.

"Hands up!" came a loud voice from inside the office.

Emily's face vanished.

Seth ran. A man leaned out the window, saw a fleeing form, leveled his pistol, and pulled the trigger. The shot exploded, the sound echoing up and down the little alleyway.

Into the bank's office stormed the men of the town, yelling and pushing at one another. A few rushed into the safe room, there to find the safe blown, while others crashed about the bank in search of thieves. Ready for anything, some carried rifles, others held pistols, and one even bore a pitchfork that he carried like a spear. The rest carried torches to light the way.

All they found was Emily Octavia Upham standing on a desk. Her tear-streaked face was as dirty as her best white pinafore. Uncombed hair streamed in all directions. Her clutched hands trembled on her chest, and her eyes, wide open with terror, saw what seemed the whole of Seth's descriptions come true—an army of bandits armed and cast in the Devil's own red by flaming torches.

When Emily saw the fifteen rifles, twelve pistols, and one pitchfork leveled at her, she uttered a soft moan and collapsed on the desk.

At the sight the men's voices instantly stilled. Then a call went up. "Get a woman in here!"

Mrs. Sedgewick, a blanket thrown over her nightdress, her long gray braid dangling behind her like a tail, swept into the room. Taking one look at the men standing around Emily, their

"Jump!" Seth yelled for the last time.

hands clutching their weapons nervously, she swooped in to protect the child.

"Air!" she cried. "Let the child have some air!"

Gathering Emily up, Mrs. Sedgewick held her on her lap like a baby as more townspeople pressed into the office. The cry of "Girl bandit!" sounded across the room and out to those who could not push their way into the bank.

Having run as fast as he could, Seth found himself safely at the edge of town. When he saw that he was not about to be caught, he circled right around again, making his way behind the houses opposite the bank. He moved forward and crawled under a porch so that he could watch what happened.

It was like election eve: the whole town was in the streets, and people were milling about, talking loudly to one another beneath the glare of torches. A new clatter sounded over the noise. Banker Upham, astride his horse, came galloping down the street. Flinging down the reins, he demounted and rushed into the bank, the crowd parting a way.

Once inside, Mr. Upham demanded to know what had happened.

"A robbery! Blew up your safe. Took everything!" people cried.

Upham nodded gravely, as he pushed through the crowd.

"But they've caught the thief!" someone shouted.

Banker Upham came to a dead stop. "What's that?" he asked, his stern look faltering.

"They've caught the crook," the man repeated.

"Come on! Make way for Mr. Upham!" someone else said.

Pushed forward against his will, Mr. Upham went into the back room. There the crowd moved away so that he saw Emily sitting on a chair, Mrs. Sedgewick by her side. When he entered the room there was a sudden hush.

Sensing that something stupendous had happened, Emily looked up. Instantly she recognized the man Seth had pointed out to her as the bandit chief. She began to weep hysterically into the sympathetic arms of Mrs. Sedgewick.

Mr. Upham took one look at the girl, then

went to inspect the safe. Satisfied that nothing was left, he returned to Emily, who had somewhat stifled her sobbing.

"What's your name?" Mr. Upham demanded.

Emily dared not look at him. "Emily Octavia Upham," she whispered in the silent room.

"Upham!" The name passed round the room.

Mr. Upham stepped back, suddenly afraid to come too close to the frightened girl.

"*What* do you call yourself?" he asked her, his voice strained.

"Emily Octavia Upham," she repeated in a bolder voice.

Mr. Upham stared at her, not at all sure what he was hearing.

A man standing by his side said, "She any relation of yours, Mr. Upham?" Some of the crowd, taking the remark as a joke, laughed.

Mr. Upham did not laugh. Puzzled, he peered down at Emily, then straightened up and looked helplessly at the crowd. They were waiting for him to do or say something.

"Ask her where she's from," called a voice.

Mechanically, Mr. Upham asked the question.

"Boston," Emily replied.

Mr. Upham, unable to think what he should do next, passed a hand through his beard.

Mrs. Sedgewick, however, was not so inhibited. "Boston, is it?" she said. "And what are you doing here?"

Emily, hearing the comforting sound of Mrs. Sedgewick's voice, turned to the woman. "I came," she said timidly, "to stay with my uncle, George P. Upham, banker of North Brookfield."

Sensation! The people in the room repeated her words to one another as if none of them had heard for themselves.

"Quiet!" roared Mr. Upham.

Instantly, silence returned.

Mr. Upham looked closely at the girl, wondering if his brother could have been fool enough to have brought his daughter along while he robbed the bank.

Mrs. Sedgewick, without waiting for Mr. Upham, asked another question on her own. "Now dear," she said, "what were you doing in the bank at this hour?"

Emily once again buried her face.

"Come, girl," said Mrs. Sedgewick, "always speak the truth."

Emily, hearing the sacred word "truth," bravely turned to the bearded man whom she believed to be the chief bandit. "We—we were taking back the money," she said.

"Robbing it, you mean!" yelled someone.

Mr. Upham silenced the man with a look. Then, very nervously, he turned back to Emily. "What," he asked, "do you mean, 'taking back'?"

"From the bandits," Emily explained.

Mr. Upham stroked his beard again, his eyes never leaving the face of the girl. He was afraid to ask her another question.

"Who's *we?*" the fatal question came from somewhere in the room. "Who was she with? Ask her that, Mr. Upham."

Mr. Upham did not want to ask her anything of the kind. He looked around helplessly.

"Go on, ask her," someone prompted.

Mr. Upham gave up. "You heard what the man said," was the best he could manage. "Who did you come with?"

"Deadwood Dick," answered Emily.

"Deadwood Dick!" The crowd was beginning to enjoy itself.

"Who's Deadwood Dick?" someone called.

Emily searched the room for the questioner. "He is a brave boy," she finally said. "We came to get money so we could go back to Boston."

"What's this Deadwood Dick look like?" someone asked.

Emily began a description as best as she was able. Halfway through it, she was interrupted by a shout: "Deadwood Dick? That's Seth Marple, that's who it is!"

Mr. Upham produced a sigh of gratitude. "Very well," he said, only too glad to accept as truth what the girl said. "When did you come to town?"

"A few days ago."

"You say," said Mr. Upham, now fully in control of himself, "that you came to see your uncle. Why, then, did you not go to him?"

"He was not at the station," explained Emily. "But Deadwood was there, and he told me that my uncle did not live nearby."

"Where have you been staying?"

"In Deadwood's house in the woods."

"And the two of you planned all this, did you?"

"No, sir, Deadwood did."

"So he's the one who took the money," pressed the banker.

"Oh, no!" exclaimed Emily. "Somebody else came and took it first!"

Someone else! The crowd flung *that* around, their excitement growing with every new bit of information. "Who was it?" The cry sounded before Mr. Upham could intervene.

"I don't know," said Emily. "I didn't see who it was."

"You expect us to believe that?" said Mr. Upham hotly.

Emily looked at him. "I *always* tell the truth."

"What about the money, Mr. Upham?" someone in the room asked. "Make her say how much Seth Marple got away with."

Mr. Upham considered the question. "I know that already," he replied. "There was four thousand dollars in that safe, in cash."

More excitement in the room. "Let's go get him then!" someone shouted, and others took up the cry.

Mr. Upham, however, remained motionless, his eyes resting on Emily. Abruptly, he turned to

Mrs. Sedgewick. "I would appreciate your keeping this girl at your home until we can determine who she really is, Mrs. Sedgewick."

This met with instant approval. Holding Emily by the hand, Mrs. Sedgewick led the girl out of the room, the men giving way to let them pass. After they had left, the townspeople followed. Mr. Upham, his mind working hard, took up the rear.

Seth, across the way under a porch, saw them swarm out of the bank. Emily looked very small in the midst of the crowd.

Mr. Upham stood at the top of the steps of the bank and waved his hand for attention. "Seth Marple!" he shouted. "He's the one we want. And I say we go get him!"

The men around Mr. Upham let out a cheer and raced for their horses.

Seth waited only long enough to see where Emily was being taken. As soon as he saw the party of women lead her to Mrs. Sedgewick's home, he decided it was time for him to leave.

The men of the town, led by Banker Upham, rushed out the east end of town, toward Seth's home. Seth, judging correctly, headed west into the woods, where he knew he would not be found. When he reached a safe spot he lay on the ground, exhausted, and soon fell asleep.

8

TRAPPED!

When Seth woke the next morning, the first thing he decided to do was to find out exactly what had happened and what had been said in the bank after he left. Emily, of course, was the only person who could tell him.

Cautiously he made his way back to North Brookfield, keeping close to the main road, but not on it, afraid that there would still be people out looking for him. Sure enough, about halfway to town he discovered Sheriff Bliss posting signs. Hiding himself until Mr. Bliss passed on, Seth inspected the nearest sign.

Wanted for Bank Robbery

SETH MARPLE

alias

DEADWOOD DICK
(*Dangerous!*)
$200 REWARD

At the bottom the bill was signed *G. P. Upham.*

Seth read the sign about twenty times. It almost made him feel proud. Deadwood Dick himself couldn't have done better. After tearing it down and stuffing it in his back pocket, he continued on his way to town.

As he walked his pride gave way to anger. And the more he thought about it, the angrier he became. Only gradually did he come to a new notion. If he caught the *real* robber, Emily's father, he would prove himself innocent and claim the reward money.

Seth reached North Brookfield without being seen. Just as easily he made his way to the back of Mrs. Sedgewick's house. There he discovered Emily sitting alone on the back porch. She was looking as clean and neat as she had when he first saw her at the station.

Using a woodpile for cover, Seth crawled toward the porch. When he got close enough, he called out, "Sssst!"

Startled, Emily looked around.

"It's me, Deadwood Dick," Seth said, showing his face around the wood.

Emily, frightened, half stood and then sat down again, smoothing out her dress nervously. She looked the other way.

"Is your jailer around?" asked Seth.

Emily, her heart beating very fast, refused to answer.

Seth crept closer. "What's the matter? Can't you talk anymore?"

"You don't tell the truth," said Emily, still not looking at him.

"What are you talking about?" he demanded.

"Your name is not Deadwood Dick. There are no bandits. My uncle does live here. You told me lies."

"Weren't lies, not really," Seth tried. "More

like stories like you read in the books, and you
have to buy *them*."

"I believed you," said Emily.

"Not my fault," insisted Seth. "Besides, I
rescued you, didn't I? I could do it again too,
right now."

Emily sat up very straight. "I don't want to be
rescued."

"You just wait," said Seth. "They're just treat-
ing you nice now. You'll see. You'll wish I had
rescued you."

For the first time Emily looked down at Seth.
"Why?" she asked, her voice fading. "What will
happen to me?"

"No, I'm not going to tell you," said Seth in
his best sulky fashion. "You just said I only tell
lies. All the same, you had better tell me what
happened after I left the bank."

Emily did not want to tell him, but Seth
coaxed it out of her. Bit by bit, he learned all that
had occurred.

"Now about that money," Seth wanted to
know. "How much did they say was stolen?"

"Four thousand dollars," said Emily. She
added, "Did you take it?"

"You were there," cried Seth. "Did you see me take it?"

"No," said Emily cautiously.

"Well, I didn't," insisted Seth. "I just wanted to get you home to your ma, like you asked me to. I'm no thief. You'll never catch me taking something like that. Not like some I could mention. 'Cause I know who *did* take the money."

"Who?" asked Emily, facing Seth squarely.

Seth looked at her. He knew that if he told her the truth she wouldn't believe him. Worse, if she *did* believe him, it would make her feel just awful.

"No," he finally said. "I can't tell you just now. But I'll find him, don't you worry about that." And without waiting for her reply, he ran off, afraid he might tell her the truth.

Emily sat for a long time after Seth had gone. Then, her mind made up, she went in to see Mrs. Sedgewick, who was busily cleaning some of Emily's things. "Mrs. Sedgewick," she began.

"Yes, child."

"Seth Marple was just here."

"Here!" the good woman cried with great fright.

"He told me he didn't take the money but he knows who did," Emily said.

Mrs. Sedgewick quickly dried her hands on her apron. "The cheek of that boy. You're not even safe from him here. I want you to tell Mr. Upham just what that dreadful boy told you!" And catching Emily by the hand, she led the way to Mr. Upham's, crying. "We must tell him right away!"

As quickly as possible, without being observed, Seth got out of town. He could not, he knew, go back to his own home. Surely, it was being watched. Nor, he decided, could he go to his hideout. Emily might have given them enough information to have found that. So he returned to the woods.

He decided, however, to go to a different place than he had been the night before, and chose to follow the creek up into the neighboring hills. There, about three miles from town, an abandoned pasture stood on higher ground than the surrounding woods. He could see if anyone was searching for him from there.

When he reached the pasture he settled his

back against a big rock and looked down over the valley toward North Brookfield. He was searching for sudden flights of birds, sure proof that people were moving through the woods. This was an Indian tactic that he had learned from his dime novels.

Seeing nothing in the direction of town to cause him concern, he turned north. Instantly he spied a thin twist of smoke rising to the sky. He knew that nobody who was searching for him would light a fire, so at first he was not worried. Then he had another thought: what if the fire had been started by Emily's father?

He looked again for the smoke, but it had already died away. He was certain, however, that he knew which direction to take in order to find it.

Trying to keep in as straight a line as possible, he moved down among the trees, but after going about a mile, he was sure that he had missed his way. Stopping, he tried to think what to do next. But even as he stood there, he smelled something: coffee.

For a long while he tried to determine exactly where the smell was coming from, but he could not. He tried listening. He heard only the occasional sound of a distant cowbell, or the sound of leaves rustling in a light breeze.

It was the breeze, however, that showed him the way. For it was carrying the smell of coffee toward him. He spat on his finger and held it in the air. The cool side told him which way the breeze was blowing. He needed only to walk into the wind. He started off immediately.

The coffee smell grew stronger. He walked so fast that he almost charged directly into the object of his search. About twenty yards in front of him, beneath a clump of pine trees, was Emily's father, fast asleep on the ground. He lay stretched out close to a fire, over which a pan of coffee was boiling. His horse, nibbling the sparse grass, was tied to a nearby stump.

For a moment Seth thought that Emily's father was dead, for he lay so very still, but a slight movement showed him to be alive. Seth took a step behind a tree, his feet crunching on dead leaves. The horse jerked its head up and flicked its ears. After a moment, it bent over the grass again.

Seth squatted down for a better look at the

sleeping man. A revolver in a holster had been hung up on a bush within easy reach. And not far from Emily's father's head was the bag in which Seth had seen him carry away the money.

Seth did not know what to do. He knew that he would not be able to capture Emily's father. Even if he tried, the man might reach out for his gun and use it on Seth. But, Seth decided, he might be able to get the money away. He looked closely to see exactly where the bag was placed.

Backing up, then taking one cautious step at a time, Seth made a big circle around the camp, ready to bolt if Emily's father awoke. The horse looked up once or twice, but paid no further attention to Seth.

Once on the opposite side of the camp, Seth began to inch closer to the sleeping man, coming up behind the bush on which the revolver was hanging. As Emily's father snored loudly, Seth reached out from behind the bush.

The horse suddenly whinnied, and Emily's father rolled over. Seth yanked back his hand, but nothing else happened.

Again Seth edged forward, reached out, and took hold of the money sack. Grasping it tightly,

The horse suddenly whinnied, and Emily's father rolled over.

he lifted it and very slowly began to back away.

Seth retreated into the woods, taking a quick look back to make sure that Emily's father was still sleeping. When he had gone about forty feet, Seth looked down at the bag more closely. It had been tied with a number of knots, but Seth decided he had better open the sack and make sure that the money was inside. He got the bag open and looked in. The money was all there.

Then Seth made another decision. He was not going to steal *anything* that he did not have a right to take. He would take the money, but *not* the bag.

Feeling virtuous, Seth dumped the money on the ground and stuffed the bag with dead leaves. When he had plumped out the bag to its previous size, he retied it, making twice as many knots as there had been before. Leaving the money heaped on the ground, he crept back to the campsite and put the money bag in the place where he had found it.

Emily's father went right on sleeping.

Going back to where the money lay, Seth attempted to gather up the pile, but it was impossible to hold all the money in his arms. Bills kept slipping to the ground. He looked around desperately for something in which to put the money. If only he had worn a shirt; the only thing he had on was his overalls. He didn't want to go back for the money bag, but he had no choice.

He turned about and took one step. A sharp whistle broke the silence. Seth looked toward the camp but saw only Emily's father stretched out on the ground. As another whistle sounded, Seth flung himself to the ground, his body covering the money. He burrowed into the leaves, hardly daring to look up. Someone was approaching the camp.

It was Banker Upham leading his own horse. With no apparent concern, he walked up to his brother, bent down, and slapped him hard. "Wake up, you fool!"

Emily's father spun about and reached for his gun. But when he saw who was standing there, he relaxed.

"You're lucky someone else didn't come upon you," said banker Upham.

"I stayed up most of the night waiting for you, but you never came," said Emily's father. He turned to the coffeepot. "It's all boiled off. What time is it?"

"Afternoon."

"You were supposed to come last night. What happened?"

"You near wrecked the whole thing," said the banker.

"What are you talking about?"

"You were seen, that's what I'm talking about."

"By whom?"

Banker Upham was so upset that he could hardly speak. First he walked one way, then another. Emily's father kept asking him what had happened.

"Don't you know?" shouted the banker.

"Of course I don't know," replied Emily's father.

"There were two kids in that bank when you blew out the safe," said the banker.

"In the bank!" Emily's father cried out.

"And one of them was your Emily!" added the banker.

"What did you say?"

"You heard me. Your Emily was in there."

Emily's father stared at the banker. "You are not serious," he said.

"I'm damn serious," insisted the banker. "What's more, she had someone with her, an obnoxious boy by the name of Seth Marple!"

"Never heard of him."

"What difference does that make!" exploded the banker. "What was that girl doing in the bank in the middle of the night? That's what I want to know."

"I don't know," said Emily's father. "I just don't know." Carefully he explained how he had left his wife and daughter in Boston without telling them what he planned to do. Suddenly he stopped. "Is my wife in town?" he asked.

"I don't think so," said his brother gloomily. "I hope not."

"What is Emily doing here, then?" cried her father.

"She says her mother put her on a train to North Brookfield. Something about a letter. I had told them not to come. Well, I didn't get any other letter, so I never met the girl at the station. But that fool of a boy did. He told her that this was bandit territory, or something like that. And it seems he promised to take her back to Boston to her mother. They were in the bank getting the train fare. I know it's ridiculous!" he yelled. "But that's what she says!"

"Beats me to nothing," admitted Emily's father.

"That's not the worst of it. It seems that while we were looking for the boy, he came to town and spoke to Emily. He told her he knows who took the money."

"How could he? He's never seen me before."

"Emily told us," said Mr. Upham, "about a hideout the boy has, north of town. That's where they've been staying. We went out and found it. Just a bunch of boards. But Emily had a picture of you and your wife there. If he's seen that— and I guess he has—then he knows you. There's bound to be trouble. The only good thing is, folks don't believe that story about another bandit. They think the boy took the money."

"Let them," said Emily's father.

"Where is the money?" asked his brother.

Emily's father reached for the bag.

"You took it all, didn't you?" asked the banker.

"Count it if you want," offered Emily's father.

"I believe you," said the banker. "But look here, if that boy knows who you are, you can't have that money. It's bound to get back to you and me. I've got to put that bag in a place where it will look like he took it." Mr. Upham held out his hand.

"I need this money," said Emily's father, drawing back.

"If you take it, you'll be in jail within a month," warned his brother. "That boy has to be found with the money on him or they'll start believing him."

Emily's father stared at the bag. Then he shrugged. "I suppose you're right," he admitted. He handed over the bag.

"Of course I am," said the banker, taking it. "You just get yourself out of here. Go back to Boston, find your wife, get yourself an alibi, and for heaven's sake, whatever you do, don't come back here. I can't have that boy see you. I'll get Emily back to Boston safe enough, don't worry about that."

Emily's father quickly packed his things, put them on his horse, and mounted. "What are you going to do now?" he asked his brother.

"I've got to hide this bag of money in the boy's house as fast as I can," said Mr. Upham. "Then I'll have the place searched and make sure it's found. He won't be able to get out of it."

"Good luck!" called Emily's father, kicking up his horse. He hurried out of the woods.

Banker Upham, holding the sack, watched his brother depart. When he was satisfied that he was gone, he started to untie the sack but found the knots too bothersome. Giving up in annoyance, he flung the bag over his horse's saddle, leaped up himself, and hurried back toward North Brookfield.

Seth had heard and seen it all.

Seth lay still where he was. He had heard the entire conversation between banker Upham and his brother, and he knew that there was only one thing for him to do. He had to get the money back to the bank without anyone seeing him do it. Only then would he be able to get out from under the banker's accusation.

Again he attempted to gather up the money. Impossible; it squirted in every direction. He considered hiding the money and going for a sack. Two things were wrong with that: it would take too much time; and worse, if he got caught, since he would be the only one who knew where the money was, they would put the blame on him for sure.

In a moment's decision he pulled off his overalls, leaving himself naked. Then he tied off the overall legs, stuffed the money into them, and rolled over the tops tightly. The money held. But it was only a temporary solution; he had to find something else in which to put the money. He couldn't stay without clothes.

Then he remembered Emily's trunk. He had hid it fairly well, he knew, and if they had not found it yet, he would be able to wrap the money in something in the trunk and so get back into his overalls. Emily, he was certain, would not miss anything. And it seemed the only thing to do, especially since the station was far enough from town so that he could get there without being seen.

Wasting no time, Seth set off down the hills

toward the railway, making extended detours to avoid meeting anyone. As it was, he reached the line three miles from the station hut, then hurried along the tracks toward it. Once a train came by, but Seth heard it long before it arrived and was easily able to hide in the bushes.

As soon as he reached the North Brookfield station, he found the trunk, big as ever, just where he had hidden it. Sweeping off branches and leaves, he lifted the top, grabbing out the dress on top. Opening his overalls, he deposited the four thousand dollars into the dress and rolled it up into a tight bundle.

With one leg in and one leg out of his overalls, he heard wagon wheels banging down into the gully. Caught by surprise, the bundle of money by his side, Seth didn't know which way to turn. The sound of voices grew louder. Afraid to run, Seth leaped into the trunk, pulling down the lid on top of him. Once inside, he burrowed beneath Emily's clothing, clutching the money.

"Where'd she say that trunk was?" said one of the two men on the wagon.

"Said they'd put it in the bushes by the station," came the answer.

Seth could hear the men tramping all about him.

"Here it is!" cried one of the men when he discovered the trunk.

"Lord, it's big," said the second man. "What's a little girl want with that big trunk?"

"Come on! Latch it up and let's get it out," said the first man. "That's what Mr. Upham said to do." The latches were snapped shut.

"Heavy cuss, ain't it?" said one of the men as they began to move it. "Them Uphams sure are rich!"

With much heaving and complaining, the men lifted the trunk, carried it to the wagon, and placed it in the back. Then they climbed on the wagon and started to move out of the gully.

Seth decided he had best get out of the trunk. Reaching up his hand, he pushed against the trunk lid. It was shut tight. He had no choice but to go along.

"Where's it going?" asked one of the men. "Mrs. Sedgwick's house?"

"Nope. Mr. Upham's got the girl up to his house. That's where it goes. She's a relation, after all."

"That Seth Marple," said the other man. "Ain't he something?"

"Mr. Upham aims to catch him and lock him up good."

"Deserves it," agreed the other.

"Says he aims to get that money back, too, if it's the last thing he does."

"If anybody can, Mr. Upham's the man."

"Four thousand dollars," said the first man. "Just before we came, I saw Mr. Upham. He'd got back from searching around the hills up North. Says he has a good notion now as to where the boy hid it."

The wagon drove on.

"If only Mrs. Marple had married Mr. Farnlee," said one of the men after a while. "Why, he might have turned the boy around."

"They say the boy don't like the preacher, and that's why she didn't."

When the wagon stopped, the men climbed down from the box. "Goes right on inside and upstairs," said one.

Carefully the trunk was taken off the wagon, and all the while complaining about its weight, the men carried it up to the second floor of Mr.

Upham's house. Then they hauled it down a hall-way and into a corner room, where it was let down.

"Yes, sir, a lot of clothes for a little girl," was their parting remark.

Seth, inside the trunk, listened carefully until he was sure that they had gone. Then he pushed hard against the lid. The trunk was still locked.

There was nothing for him to do but wait. Tired from having little sleep the night before, he fell asleep, using the bundle of money for a pillow.

· 9 ·

BY DARK OF NIGHT!

Seth woke with a start at the sound of voices. He recognized them instantly. The first voice belonged to Emily, the second was that of banker Upham himself.

"You may stay here, Emily," Mr. Upham was saying, "until I write to your father in Boston. Then I must send you back home."

"Thank you, Uncle," said Emily.

"And don't you worry," continued Mr. Upham. "That boy shan't bother you here. We'll catch him soon enough in any case. Will this room suit you?"

"It's very nice," said Emily.

"We've fetched all your things from that boy's place in the woods. And there's your trunk, so now you have everything. Is there anything else that you might need?"

"I am fine," said Emily.

"Now don't you worry about anything," the banker told her. "You're not to blame. You will never have to see that scoundrel again. I've an excellent idea where the money is and we'll go get it. Dinner will be ready in an hour. Please come down then."

"Thank you, Uncle."

Mr. Upham turned to go.

"Uncle," called Emily.

"Yes, what is it?" he asked.

"I don't think the boy took the money."

"I know better than you do," said Mr. Upham severely. "Don't speak of it again. Please get dressed for dinner." So saying, he left the room.

Sadly Emily watched him go. She looked about the corner room with its blue wallpaper, bed in the center, a dresser, and curtained windows. Her trunk was up against the wall.

By her bedside she got down on her knees and began to pray. "Bless Papa," she began softly, "who went to find some money. Forgive him for saying *that* word. Bless Mama in her sister's house. I hope she comes to get me soon. Bless my Uncle Upham for finding me and saving me." Emily paused, deep in thought. "And bless the boy, wherever he is. He lied to me and did terrible things. But I do not think he meant to do anything bad. Teach him to be a good Christian. I don't think he took the money. I don't. Please help him get far, far away."

Listening to it all, Seth decided that Emily was in the right mood. Cautiously he tapped on the trunk lid. Emily, still on her knees, turned around at the sound.

"Emily," called Seth. "It's me, Deadwood."

"Where are you?"" called Emily in a frightened voice.

"Here, in your trunk."

After a moment's hesitation, Emily opened the catches on the trunk and lifted the lid. There was Seth, grinning broadly. For a moment Emily just stared at him, then she ran to the door of the room and closed it.

"What are you doing here?" she whispered, leaning against the door.

"Taking a nap," Seth explained, making sure the bundle of money was well out of sight.

"How did you get here?"

"I can't rightly explain it," said Seth modestly. "And I'm sorry to have messed up your clothing. Had to be," he assured her, climbing out of the trunk.

Emily put her hand to the doorknob. "I must tell my uncle!"

"Don't!" cried Seth.

"I must!"

"Didn't you just say in your prayers that I didn't take the money? And didn't you know I was telling the truth? Said it to God, didn't you? Well, you can say it to me."

Emily only stared at him.

"Okay, then, it's true," Seth said. "I swear to God. I didn't take the money. But, like I told you, I know who did."

"Who?"

Seth looked into Emily's frightened eyes. "I'm not sure I should say."

"I can't believe you unless you tell me," she pleaded.

Seth considered how to tell her the truth.

"What are you doing here?" she whispered, leaning against the door.

"Well," he said carefully, "his last name is *Upham*."

"My uncle!" cried Emily, her eyes wide.

"I guess his name is Upham," agreed Seth.

"How do you know?"

"Well, for one thing, I saw him in the bank during the night," Seth obliged, pleased with the way the explanation was working out.

"People don't steal their own money," Emily said after a moment.

"I agree," said Seth. "It doesn't seem right. But there it is. And you said it was your Uncle, not me."

Emily's face was very pale. "But that would not be honest."

"Sure isn't. Worse than that, he's telling everybody *I* stole it. Well, I'll tell you one thing, and this is as true as true ever can be. You can believe me when I say that the money is right here in this house!"

Emily's eyes grew very wide. "Where?"

"Oh," said Seth, casually. "Somewhere. I know that."

Emily sat on the edge of her bed, breathing

heavily. "My uncle said you stole my mama's letter and that's why he didn't meet me at the train."

"Now there's a lie!" protested Seth. "He's got more lies than a dog has fleas. Stealing letters! I never did and I can swear to that. Ask the sheriff. You think I'd do anything like that?"

Emily sniffed. "No," she said. "I don't."

"Well, there you are."

"What shall we do?" asked Emily anxiously.

"You go on down to your dinner," suggested Seth. "When you come back, bring some food up here for me. I don't think I've eaten anything in a week. But you won't go and tell him, will you?"

"I won't," she whispered. "I promise I won't."

Emily shut the trunk lid over Seth while she changed her clothes and got ready for dinner. After listening to his repeated warnings not to say *anything,* she left, shutting the door behind her.

As soon as she was gone, Seth climbed out of the trunk, eased open the door, and watched her go down the steps to the main floor. Then he ran back to the trunk and hauled out the bundle of money.

Holding the bundle under his arm, he listened, looked up and down the hall, then stepped out of the room as quietly as he could. The house was as grand as anything he had ever seen. A careful look in the passage, however, revealed no place in which to put the money. He went to the steps and looked down. He couldn't see Emily and her uncle. They must be eating in another part of the house. He could barely hear the clink of plates and silver.

He started down the steps, the bundle under his arm. Halfway down he stopped, listening, trying to make sure that they were in fact in another part of the house. Mr. Upham seemed to be doing all the talking.

At the bottom of the steps was Mr. Upham's black account box with its brass lock. The key was in the lock.

Mr. Upham's voice boomed out: "That boy is as evil as they come!"

Seth went over to the box, turned the key, and lifted the lid. The box was full of papers. These Seth removed. Then he took the bundle, unwrapped it, and slid all the money into the box. Closing the lid, he locked it and put the key in his pocket.

Seth went back to Emily's room and looked at the papers he had removed from the box. They were bills, bills and accounts. Seth stuffed them under the mattress of Emily's bed.

Then he checked the window, opening it in case he had to leave quickly. Having done that, he went back to the trunk and pulled the lid down over him.

There was no need for a quick escape. Emily played true; she even brought some food with her, which Seth ate ravenously.

"Did you tell?" he asked her.

She shook her head no, her eyes never leaving him.

"Thanks," he said.

"You have awful manners," Emily said, thinking she had to let him know.

"Guess I do," he agreed. Emily was silent.

"My uncle said he is getting a warrant to search your house tomorrow morning."

Seth stopped eating. "What's a warrant?" he asked.

"It is permission to search your house for the money," Emily answered.

"Permission from who?" demanded Seth, angrily.

"A judge."

"What's he expect to find in my house?" Seth asked.

"He said the money you took will be there. Is it?"

"I told you. It's here in *this* house."

Emily sat quietly while Seth resumed eating. "What are you going to do?" she finally asked.

"Nothing to worry about. Deadwood Dick knows what to do."

"Please do not say that name," Emily pleaded. "It is not yours."

"Beats out Seth Marple any day," Seth told her, finishing up his food, and to Emily's disgust wiping his hands on his overalls.

"Look here," said Seth suddenly. "There's something I want you to do."

Emily said nothing.

Seth pulled Mr. Upham's key out of his pocket and held it out to her. "I want you to take special care of this."

"What is it for?" Emily asked.

"Never mind what. You just keep it and don't give it to *anyone* excepting if I tell you to. Can you promise that?"

After a moment of thought Emily silently took the key. Seth stood up.

"Where will you go tonight?" Emily asked.

Seth looked about the room. By the side of Emily's bed was the Bible he had given her, Mr. Farnlee's Bible.

"I'm going to see the preacher," he said.

Emily's face brightened. "Are you?"

"Didn't I just say so? Only I need one thing. Can I borrow that Bible I gave you?"

Emily jumped to her feet and happily bestowed the book upon Seth. "You may have it," she said with tears in her eyes. "You *are* a good boy."

Taking it, Seth felt the worst ever.

As soon as it was dark enough Seth climbed out the second floor window, the Bible stuffed in his overalls. Sliding down the drainpipe, he quickly reached the ground. He ran from Thistle Hill, where Mr. Upham lived, to the house next to the church, where Mr. Farnlee lived. There was a light in the window.

Seth sneaked around to the back door. Holding the Bible behind his back, he knocked.

Mr. Farnlee opened the door. "What are you doing here!" he cried, pulling Seth inside and shutting the door behind him. "The whole county is out looking for you!"

"Well, I'm right here, I guess," Seth answered.

"And your poor mother," scolded the preacher as he went around the room hastily drawing the curtains, "how can you treat her so cruelly?"

"I guess I wasn't meaning to," Seth replied.

"Have you no love for her?"

"Sure I do."

"Robbing banks!" cried Mr. Farnlee. "Kidnaping a young lady from Boston. Seth Marple, you are Satan's own!"

"I didn't do any of that," said Seth stoutly.

"You needn't lie to me, young man!"

"I didn't," Seth insisted. "None of it. But I know who did rob the bank."

"What sort of nonsense are you talking?"

"That's what I came to see you about," Seth told him. "I thought you would listen, seeing as my ma is my ma, if you know what I mean."

Mr. Farnlee started to speak but changed his mind. Instead, his face grew very red.

"All I know," continued Seth, "is that they don't come any more innocent than I am. But there is a thief in this town, and I can catch him, sure enough."

Mr. Farnlee thrust a chair at Seth. "You had better sit down and tell me what this is all about."

Seth, the Bible still behind his back, remained standing. "That's just what I was meaning to do," he said, studying the floor. "The point is, you want to marry my ma, don't you?"

"Your mother is the finest of women," said the preacher. "I did offer her my hand in marriage, but . . . but . . ."

"But what?" asked Seth, afraid to look up.

The preacher cleared his throat. "God does not will it."

"I guess I don't follow you," said Seth.

"The Lord," said Mr. Farnlee with some difficulty, "presumed to give us a sign that it would be wrong to contemplate such an action. Who am I to question the ways of the Lord?"

Seth held his breath for a moment, then pulled Mr. Farnlee's Bible out from behind his back. "I—I think this is yours," he said quietly, unable to look up.

"*Where did you get that!*" cried the preacher, snatching it from Seth's hand.

"Well, I guess you might say I took it," said Seth, managing to raise his eyes a bit.

The preacher stood taller and straighter than Seth had ever seen him before. "I demand an explanation!" said Mr. Farnlee.

Haltingly, Seth told him what he had done, how he had not meant to go to his house, how he had not meant to spy on anybody, how he had not mean to do anything wrong, and how he had not meant to be cruel or mean, but that somehow, *some way,* it just worked out like that.

"I'm awful sorry you took it the wrong way," said Seth. "I just wanted to tell you the Lord didn't take the Bible at all. It was just me, Seth Marple."

The preacher listened in unsmiling silence. When the boy had finished, he said, "Why are you telling me this?"

" 'Cause I have to tell someone the truth about what's happening, so I figured if I started by telling you the truth about the Bible, you would believe me."

The preacher remained erect. "We shall have to see. You may begin your story. Please tell me everything. *All* of it."

So Seth told him the entire story from start to finish, leaving out no detail, for better or for worse. At the conclusion he added: "Only I don't want Emily to know it was her pa. You don't know how she sobs. She'd never stop if she lived to be a hundred if she knew."

Mr. Farnlee seemed to relax. He paced a bit, then came back to stare down at the boy. "You are a dreadful rascal, Seth Marple."

"Yes, sir, I guess I am."

"But why should the Upham brothers want to steal their own money?" Mr. Farnlee asked, as much to himself as to Seth.

"I guess," offered Seth, "if they were going to steal, they were going to have to steal from themselves. There ain't anybody else in town who you *can* steal money from."

Then the preacher did something that Seth had never seen him do before. He laughed. Seth laughed, too, even if he didn't quite see the joke.

"A search warrant was issued," the preacher said suddenly. "We are to search your house first thing tomorrow morning."

"I guess we'll find something," Seth agreed. "But it ain't going to be that money."

After writing a brief letter to Seth's mother, which he gave to Seth, Mr. Farnlee told the boy that he was to sneak home, making absolutely certain that he was not caught. Seth was never so happy to do as he was told.

Mrs. Marple was overjoyed to see him. She hugged him and cried over him, and even Seth knew he rather liked it. Then she read Mr. Farnlee's letter but would not show it to Seth. Whatever it was, it seemed to make her feel better. She even patted Seth on the head and called him a "good boy," something he had not heard for a long, long time.

She then told Seth to go to bed, which he did,

at least for a few moments. As soon as she wasn't watching, he slipped out, just to see where Mr. Upham had put the bag of leaves that he thought contained the money. Seth found it easily, under the house. His mother had told him that Mr. Upham had come around just that afternoon.

Seth returned to his bed, this time to sleep soundly.

EMILY UPHAM'S REVENGE!

The next morning Seth got up early, not wanting to miss anything that was going to happen. His mother fixed breakfast, which he allowed was the best food he had eaten in a long time, not excepting what Emily had given him up on Thistle Hill.

Then he went out on the front steps, gathered up his Deadwood Dick books, and started to read. But somehow they didn't seem very interesting. He kept looking down the road.

He did not have long to wait.

He heard a clatter and beheld the sight he had

been waiting for. It was the preacher's wagon. Mr. Farnlee was driving up the road. In the wagon with him were Sheriff Bliss and Mr. Upham. Wedged in between was Emily.

They drove up to the door and stopped.

Mr. Upham leaped from the wagon. "Sheriff!" he cried. "I want that boy arrested. You've got the authority."

"We'll get to it, we'll get to it," said Sheriff Bliss. "There's nothing but the truth going to happen here today. I've taken my oath to that."

Emily, who kept stealing glances at Seth, looked very pale. Seth only grinned back at her.

Mr. Upham turned back to the wagon and fetched out his black accounts box. When Seth saw him do it, he had to bite his lips to keep from laughing.

Sheriff Bliss approached the door. "Young man, is your mother to home?"

"Sure is," Seth answered.

The sheriff knocked, and Mrs. Marple came to the door. After an exchange of greetings, Sheriff Bliss began the proceedings.

"You'll excuse me, ma'am," he said, pulling a document out of his pocket. "But I have here a

warrant to search your house. What we're looking for is four thousand dollars, believed to be
stolen by this here boy, who goes by the name of
Seth Marple, alias Deadwood Dick."

"Didn't do it!" Seth threw in.

Mrs. Marple looked toward the preacher.
When he nodded slightly, she said, "Please come
in." The entire party entered.

Seth found it fun to watch. Mr. Upham and
Sheriff Bliss searched all through the little house.
No one found anything. All the while that the
search was going on, Emily sat perfectly still, her
hands clasped in her lap.

Then Mr. Upham said, "Sheriff Bliss, I can
look under the house, can't I?"

Sheriff Bliss said that he could.

"Would you help me look there?" asked the
banker.

And Sheriff Bliss did, of course. Everybody
went along, Emily included.

Mr. Upham walked right up to the spot, bent
over, and cried, "What's that in there, Mr.
Bliss?"

Mr. Bliss, ever obliging, dragged out the bag.

"Why, that is the bag that held the money

in the safe at the bank," asserted Mr. Upham.

"Then we had best open it up," said the sheriff.

They brought the bag into the house, and everybody crowded around it. Mr. Bliss started working on the knots, but there were so many that this took him some time, which made everybody very impatient. At last he untied the last knot.

"Dump it out!" demanded Mr. Upham. "And I want a full counting of everything in there!"

"Certainly. Certainly," agreed Mr. Bliss. Lifting up the bag, he turned it over. Out spilled the leaves.

"He has that money somewhere!" roared Mr. Upham.

Mr. Farnlee stepped forward. "Just a moment, Mr. Upham. Seth Marple, since you stand accused, have you anything to say about this?"

"I guess I do," said Seth, accepting his cue. "I never said I wasn't in the bank. Don't deny that. But I didn't steal anything. It was someone else. It was Mr. Upham, that's who!"

Mr. Upham turned purple. "It's a damned lie!" he screamed. "Nothing but a damned lie!"

Emily, horrified at *that* word, clapped her hands over her ears.

"How could I steal my own money?" continued Mr. Upham. "And if I did, where is it?"

"Why," said Seth, nice and easy, "I saw you put it in your black box."

"Another lie!" screamed Mr. Upham. "A terrible lie." And fetching up his black box, he dropped it on the table. "You may open it if you wish. I dare you!"

Seth turned to Emily and held out his hand. "I need the key," he said.

Her hand trembling, Emily took the key out of one of her gloves and gave it to the boy. When Mr. Upham saw what was happening, his eyebrows shot up. But it was too late.

"May I?" said Mr. Farnlee, taking the key from Seth. He placed the key in the lock, twisted it, and flipped open the lid. Everybody pressed around to look.

The box was empty.

"I told you!" cried Mr. Upham. "It is that boy who is the thief!"

"He stole the money," accused Seth.

"Stop!" thundered Mr. Farnlee over the

shouts of everybody else. Then he turned severely upon Seth. "Seth Marple," he demanded, "what is happening here?"

"I'm sure I don't know," Seth admitted.

"I insist that you arrest that boy," said Mr. Upham to the sheriff.

"Nope. Can't do it without evidence," returned Mr. Bliss. "We have to find the money first. And we ain't found it, have we?"

Everybody began talking at the same time. Everybody but Emily. She had retreated into a corner of the room where she stood alone. She was still standing there when Seth noticed her.

Suddenly he understood.

He banged on the table until people stopped talking. Then he turned to her. "Emily," said Seth, "I suppose you don't know anything about this, do you?"

Emily, her eyes bright, appeared not to have heard what Seth said.

The boy came closer. "Emily," he repeated. "I guess you *do* know something."

Emily stared at Seth.

Mr. Upham suddenly became frightened. "What have you done, girl?"

Seth watched Emily carefully, expecting her to close her eyes and count to fifteen. But she didn't. Instead she looked at all the people who were looking at her, and—or so it seemed to Seth—something like a fierce look came into her eyes.

"It's gone," she said simply.

"Gone!" screamed the banker.

"Gone!" cried Seth.

"Gone," echoed Emily faintly.

Seth, suddenly remembering, cried out in horror: "I bet you burned it. That's what you said you would do. You've burned it!"

"Burned four thousand dollars!" yelled Mr. Upham.

Emily only looked at Seth with sad eyes, as everybody began to talk at once.

"Let the girl speak!" demanded Mr. Farnlee loudly. "Now," he continued when all was quiet, "what we want to know, Emily, what we *need* to know, is two things. Where did you find that money, and, did you burn it?"

Emily considered her answer for a long time, her eyes moving from Seth to her uncle Upham. When she spoke, she spoke quietly but firmly.

"I cannot tell a lie," she managed to say. "But I will not tell the truth, either."

"My God!" said Mr. Upham. "She *did* burn it!"

There was nothing else to do. No matter how much they tried to get Emily to speak, she absolutely refused to say another word.

Later that day, Mr. Farnlee had a private word with Mr. Upham in the bank. He said that while *he* did not believe it, Seth Marple had told him "about a certain meeting in the woods between two brothers whose names I do not wish to mention. Furthermore—"

Banker Upham interrupted hastily. "No need to discuss the matter," he said. "As far as I am concerned, the entire business is closed." He held the door open for Mr. Farnlee to leave.

After the preacher had gone, Mr. Upham returned to his chair and stared at a blank wall for the better part of an hour.

That evening, when her uncle Upham returned to his home on Thistle Hill, Emily was waiting for him. She arose to greet him as he entered the house.

"I cannot tell a lie," she managed to say.
"But I will not tell the truth, either."

Banker Upham looked sternly at her. "You have done an awful thing," he said. "I am packing you off to Boston as soon as possible. I have already sent a wire to your parents."

"Uncle," said Emily, unmoved. "I wish to see Seth Marple once more."

"Whatever for?" her uncle asked.

"I wish to see him," she repeated.

Something in the way Emily looked at him made Mr. Upham feel uneasy. "Very well. You may do so," he said. "But it must be brief." So saying, he left the room.

Seth answered Emily's summons the next morning. Ushered into the main room of Mr. Upham's house, he found Emily sitting in a large chair by the fireplace. She was ready to leave for Boston, and her parasol and traveling bag were at her side.

"They said you wanted to see me," She began.

"I did."

"All that money," said Seth, shaking his head. "It was an awful thing to do."

"That is just what Uncle Upham said to me," she answered.

Stung, Seth hung his head. "Well, it was," he tried.

"You told all those lies," she said to him. "I think you put that money in the box even if you didn't steal it."

Seth, feeling more and more uncomfortable, said nothing.

"Money," continued Emily, "is the root of all evil."

"That's all right then," retorted Seth with a grin. "I don't have any money to speak of."

Emily suddenly got out of her chair and came up close to Seth. "Who did come to the bank that night?" she whispered.

Seth, not wanting to look at her, tried to step away, but she held on to his arm. "You don't want to know," he insisted.

"I do."

"You don't."

"I have to know," she said, holding his arm tighter.

"Well, then, it was your pa, that's who."

Sighing, Emily closed her eyes. When she opened them again, tears shone there. Still holding his arm, she suddenly pulled him down and kissed him on the cheek. "You are a good boy," she whispered.

Seth, not knowing what to do, waited for her to say something further. When she didn't, he mumbled goodbye and left.

In Boston, Emily was met at the station by Polly.

"I forgive you for what you said about my house," cried Polly, hugging the girl warmly. "And I'll take you to your own home now." She then offered to carry Emily's things.

Emily, stoutly insisting upon taking her own parasol and traveling bag, stepped quickly into the waiting cab.

At home, Emily found both parents waiting for her.

"Are you better, mama?" Emily asked, as her mother wept over her.

"Your papa is home, so of course I am better," her mother replied.

Emily turned to her father. "Papa, did you get the money you needed?"

"Not yet," he admitted with a shrug. "I suppose we'll have to sell this house. But don't worry. We shall manage."

"Papa?"

"Yes, my dear."

"Were you in Uncle Upham's bank that night?"

"Me?"

"Seth said you were."

Emily's father turned away. He went to the far side of the room, where he pulled at his mustache. "Is Seth that dreadful boy who kidnapped you?" he asked.

"Were you in the bank, Papa?" Emily asked urgently.

"Now, Emily," he tried. "That is nothing for little girls to discuss."

"Please, you *must* tell me!"

"What is she talking about?" demanded Emily's mother.

"I have not the slightest idea," insisted Mr. Upham.

"Papa tried to steal the money," said Emily.

"That is a *damned* lie!" cried her father.

"You did, you did," sobbed Emily. "But I

shall never, never, *never* tell!'' And snatching up her parasol and traveling bag, she ran to her room and locked the door.

Mrs. Marple did marry Mr. Farnlee. She and Seth moved to the house next door to the church. There, Seth hid his dime novels in the attic, where he continued to read them. His new father knew this quite well. But then, Seth did not complain of the preacher's sermons on the plight of the South Seas heathen.

As for Mr. George P. Upham, banker, he blamed the whole affair on North Brookfield's not having a railway line directly into town. His committee therefore proposed a route for such a line, as well as a grand new station. The upper floor of this station was to be used to house a temperance society, to be placed under the direction of Mr. Farnlee.

There is only one more thing to tell.

That night, the night when Emily fled to her room and locked the door, she opend her traveling bag. Out of it she took four thousand dollars and hid it in a safe place. Each week at church she placed a sealed white envelope containing some of the bills into the charity box. In time all the money was gone.

And so, after all is said and done, only North Brookfield's new station remains, a monument to *Emily Upham's Revenge.*